# Post-trip

**Sydney Pelletier**

**Kids**
Kitty and Company
King Sunny and the Rainbow
The Little Book of Halloween
Ready for Christmas
The Wizard and the Star
My First Valentine
Mimi on the Move


**Adults**
Overdose
Post-trip
School Break
Bloopers on Paper
Obsidian Drones
Ex Nihilo
Intercession

1

I can't get up. This morning, it's impossible. I've hit "snooze" about fifteen times already. Funny thing is, I'm actually ecstatic: my school career is expiring. Today is the first day of my very last university trimester. It barely feels like it's real, but it is. In one hundred and five days exactly, total freedom. Four classes, twelve hours every week, for fifteen weeks – and that's it! Yes sir! No more school!!

Something stops me from getting up. I'm happy, yes, except it's like I'm on standby. When I think about other students, especially new students – those who just bought loads of notebooks and exercise books, binders and plaid pencil cases – I actually get guilt pangs. I know I've paid my dues, but still. After seventeen years spent in or around schools (ten uneventful, two decisive, two back-breaking and now almost three mortal ones), it's clear I have to move on. It's actually urgent. My tolerance for anything academic is on a steep decline, a downgraded appeal easily summarized in one simple sentiment: saturation. I've had enough of wading through boring classes, of collecting bad grades or struggling to get better ones, of downloading useless info, getting lost in libraries, documenting myself while staying objective, of analysing and counter-analysing, dissecting topics I don't care about, half-processing everything while dodging an endless onslaught of spelling mistakes. No, that's it. I've had enough of school.

I sit up in bed.  While I was sleeping, I sent the bedsheets flying, somehow.  It was my father who insisted I went to university.  I, on the other hand, was quite prepared to phase-out my student career right after high school.  I could've gone on working leisurely at the Community Center, full-time instead of part-time, like I do now.

I get out of bed.  My clothes are cold; underwear, bra, pants, sweater – everything's frozen stiff.  What a terrible way to wake up.  My father didn't care what field of studies I chose, just as long as I was registered someplace in something.  I had to choose and so I chose "Literature".  I thought it would be fun.  Of course, big giant monumental mistake.  Literature is definitely not fun, not for me anyway.  I don't know why exactly.  I think I'd rather hand out day-coupons at the Community Center for a week than figure out why.  And that's saying something.  Worst thing is, when I first got admitted into the program, I was actually delighted, very self-satisfied.  But now, after twenty-six classes of cramming everything in and typing everything out, always trying to get my hands on that ever elusive bachelor's degree, I'm ready to quit.  Sure, I know, it's way too late to turn back now, and also, it's a matter of pride to get the thing done, even though I now know, without the slightest shadow of a doubt, that Literature is way, way out of my depth.

Now I'm late.  I've wasted too much time thinking about stuff instead of getting breakfast.  After ingesting two pancakes (folded, to save time), I drive my old car down to the train station.  Living in the west-end of Montreal (aka "the West Island") makes commuting inevitable.  I'd love to just drive straight downtown, and from there to school, but it's impossible: there's never any parking anywhere and, what with traffic and/or traffic jams, it just costs too much gas overall.

Like any typical suburban area, the West Island glories in its reputation for being strictly residential, with big houses and big lawns. This means that means of public transportation are few and far between. The nearest bus stop stands thirty minutes from any known civilization, and buses stop there once every hour. That's on average. Getting downtown without packing a lunch and a tent is an occupational hazard. To bypass this, I drive halfway to the city, then take the train and then the metro to complete the journey. On a round-trip, the shortcut takes about three hours. No kidding.

This morning's no different: after a near-collision with a cyclist, a lopsided parallel-parking and a pancake-resurfacing dash, I miraculously catch the train. Inside the passenger car, it happens: I'm hit full in the face by a familiar kind of rancid air. It's funny. Even though it's throat-pinching awful, I've gotten used to that train smell, I've learned to recognize it as something reassuring, something that almost belongs to me. With it, I also get a fresh flush of nerves: I know this is my last session, that I'm graduating soon, but today's still a first day of school. The first last day of school. It's still stressful.

The train car gets underway. I walk the length of the aisle, looking for my usual spot. In the near distance, I can see the ticket-controller. Since I don't know the man's name, I've been mentally referring to him, whenever such a calamity occurs, as "Ticket-Ticket". I can see him now, smiling spontaneously when he catches sight of me. I almost feel like traipsing over there, swatting him on the shoulder and shrieking joyfully "This is my last session, ever!!!" before kissing his jolly rosy cheeks, but his big handlebar mustache, complete with wriggling whiskers, cuts off my enthusiasm at the source. Instead I limit my response to a nice, polite smile, and sit down with no welcome signal whatsoever. Ticket-Ticket ambles over anyway while I rummage through my bag, looking for a book to munch on:

"Hello, Miss Laurie!"

I look at him. His mustache stretched over a permanent grin, Ticket-Ticket stands over me, merrily wide-eyed. For three years now, he's been calling me "Miss Laurie". Not once have I called him anything. Still, it never misses. Every time, he clicks into the same routine; leaning on the bench in front of me, he plants one foot behind the other and tucks his hands on his hips. In spite of looking very formal in his navy-blue uniform, Ticket-Ticket doesn't check my fare; he knows I buy a monthly pass. No, his sole purpose for standing here is to shoot the breeze. I usually muster enough patience to bear the weight of his presence until the next stop, but even though I visibly strain throughout, Ticket-Ticket's clueless. He thinks I like him. Dear man. Under his controller cap, his basset-face just hangs there, beaming with the unbridled enthusiasm that goes with the species. This morning, because I'm in a good mood, I manage to reciprocate:

"Hi. How are you?"

"Ah, Miss Laurie… Long time no see!"

"Yes, that's true."

We have the same polite exchange every September; the words flow effortlessly between us, which is strangely comforting.  With the rough edge of his little notepad, Ticket-Ticket scratches around his collar before throwing me his next question:

"You're off to school now?"

"Yes, I am."

"It's good to be in school.  Getting an education is important."

"Yes, it is."

Ticket-Ticket smiles.  A sudden jolt on the tracks momentarily destabilizes him.  He has no reaction to speak of: his kind eyes still on me, he absorbs the shockwave like jelly and carries on.

"My son, the youngest, he just started school last week."

"Really?"

"Yep, he's in kindergarten.  He was so excited, on his first morning he threw up all his little cereals."

I smile rigidly as two half-digested pancakes come to mind.  Ticket-Ticket continues, his voice unctuous with tenderness.

"Poor little thing.  He's in love with his teacher. He goes on and on: "Mrs. Lewis said this, Mrs. Lewis said that!"  That's all we hear back home."

The train slows down and stops at a station. Ticket-Ticket pricks up his ears, on high alert as passengers start to file in.

"Well, I'm off to work.  Have a nice day, Miss Laurie."

"Thank you.  Have a nice day."

With one last mustache twirl, Ticket-Ticket turns on his heels, calling out "Ticket!… Ticket!!!" over the din.

Back to my book. I try to immerse myself in the story but my thoughts wander. Facing me now are four months of shuttling back and forth between the West Island and the city. The train tracks run through a long stretch of nothingness alongside Highway 20. There's no view. I just hope I've picked the "right" spot to sit at this morning. On the train, everyone always sits approximately in the same place, in the same passenger car. One misguided choice and commuting can suddenly become a descent into hell on wheels. Take last year's cream of the crop, for example:

On Mondays, behind me: a lady mushily chewing her melon bubble gum right in my ear.

On Wednesdays, out front: a gentleman breathing too loud.

On Thursdays, behind me again: a skinny girl munching on a breakfast of BBQ chips.

And on Fridays, opposite me: a woman loudly trimming her fingernails with a dull clipper.

Okay, so I know I could've moved instead of complaining about all these people, but I'm equal parts impatience and stubbornness. I try to make an effort, I really do, but I can't help it; I struggle with public transport. What I need, is private transport.

I make landfall five train stations and ten metro stations later. Walking to class, I check someone's watch; I'm on time. This morning, I have a Poetry workshop. I usually like workshops. I'm not that good at poetry, but workshops have a fun, relaxed atmosphere, very conducive to spirited exchanges. There's that "one big family" feeling that puts students more at ease – and in school, a comfortable, motivated student is always a precious commodity.

Stepping inside the classroom, I take the first vacant seat in sight, right next to a pretty raven-haired girl; she's reading a book distractedly, one elbow crumpling the pages, one hand cupping her chin. After noticing the name of the author on the cover, I ask:

"Is it any good?"

An easy introduction, very simple, just to make contact. The girl bolts upright and smiles at me shyly:

"Oh, yes, it's fantastic!"

It's imperceptible, or barely perceptible, but her whole demeanor has changed: she's sitting with her back very straight now, her hands respectfully stroking the book, conscientiously perusing its pages, all of a sudden. That's weird. It's almost like she felt threatened by my questi…

"You didn't read it?!!?"

That came out of left field – literally. Turning to my left, I'm confronted with two enormous eyes magnified by thick trifocal glasses. I inquire:

"What?"

"I said "You didn't read it?" How is that even possible?"

The guy who's talking to me now is actually sincere; he's astounded by my limited erudition. Oh God, he's right. I don't belong here, I should never have come here without reading the book the girl on my right is no longer reading because she's waiting to hear what I'll answer to the guy on my left, still bulging behind his glasses. Although intimidated, I reply honestly:

"No, I haven't read it."

And the rebuttal comes, in a scandalized tone:

"But it's the masterpiece of one of the world's greatest authors!"

I smile here. A little because of misplaced embarrassment, a little because I was expecting as much. I'll admit it because it's true; my culture is very plebeian. In the summer, when I don't have to read essays on intertextuality or narratology, I read comics. Or comic books, if I'm really on a roll. Now, confronted with the obvious, and left with whatever courage and dignity I can spare, I keep words to a minimum:

"It's a masterpiece? I see."

The guy stares at me, still appalled behind his glasses. When he turns away, evidently disgusted, the girl on my right reverts to type and reads in silence again. I open my bag and take out a few sheets of paper. When the teacher enters the classroom, I feel all right, even proud of myself: in the space of two minutes, I've managed to meet two people whose notes I'll probably have to borrow when I'll skip class. If I had to choose now, I'd go for Trifocals' notes, right off the bat: our class hasn't even started yet, and already my pretty raven-haired neighbor is busy doodling neurotic flowers in her notebook. As my only alternative, Trifocal's dry, cold-surgery notes (as I'm sure he takes them) will have to do.

Class begins. The teacher, a tall lady dressed in purple from head to toe, gives us a brief account of her academic curriculum, just as a lead-in. It's a nice overture, nothing special; I'm even tempted to think things are looking up. Until she hands us the program.

Many faces fall as the teacher strolls between rows, passing out her syllabus and calling us "my friends" at the same time. Trifocals smiles when he gets his copy. When I get mine, I immediately spot "Participation: 40%" in the evaluation section. My throat constricts as I read on: "Every student must read <u>in front of the class</u> a poem of his or her own composition, which will then be critiqued by his or her peers."

Under the desk, my legs liquefy. Over the desk, there's a shortage of ambient air. I read and reread the words again: "<u>in front of the class</u>". There they are, in black and white – underlined.

Many students, who feel as I do, raise their hands to protest, telling the teacher she's lumping us all in the same category (the category of real poets who feel the vital need to read their creations out loud in front of everybody else).

"I'm sorry, my friends, but no one writes to be forgotten."

That's the teacher's ruling right there. Her kind but decisive tone closes the matter. In the next few seconds, all the students with whom I could've commiserated about my desire to leave, leave. That leaves me alone, stranded on my island of anxiety, with the girl on my right still doodling and Trifocals on my left still smiling because he has clones of himself among what remains of our class. We are now twelve in a workshop that was supposed to accommodate thirty. I'm desperate to get out of here but it's not like I have a choice: I need this class to get my degree. I look at my old pencil case, yawning on the desk in front of me. Two ball-point pens and a flabby eraser protrude between the square teeth of the zipper. The teacher starts talking again but her voice only reaches me in broken-up snatches. I'm still staring at my pencil case, floating out of myself, at present incapable of paying any attention to anything else. I'm petrified. For me, an oral presentation is an open war, an impossible battle with only two possible outcomes: to die (doing the presentation) or to survive (not doing the presentation, flunking out and then pretending I don't care). An oral presentation makes me ill, even the prospect of it. Months in advance.

As I slowly re-emerge, the teacher sits down behind her desk and selects the dates of our poem read-alouds. Already!?! My God. Presentations are spread over the next few weeks; my own execution is scheduled for early October – three Mondays from now, in less than a month. I feel really bad. I think I'm getting nauseous when the teacher starts her class on André Breton and his caboodle of surrealists. I *know* I'm nauseous by the time she tackles Paul Éluard. That's it: I'll be sick with anticipation for a whole month, dreading the big moment with an odd assortment of heart palpitations and stomach ulcers. The teacher, meanwhile, is still smiling widely. She hits us head-on with an exercise: before we leave today, she wants us to write an "automatic poem", an improvised sonnet composed this instant, at the double, "Just to see what's in your guts this morning", she says, laughing. I already know what's in my guts; acid-refluxed pancakes (my esophagus is burning like hell). Quickly, quickly, I write a pitiful little poem that doesn't even rhyme. After a few moments, the teacher calls out to us kindly:

"Everybody done? All right. Now, I want you to exchange compositions. Sharing your poem with someone else is still part of the writing process."

I immediately turn to the girl on my right, but she's already traded poems with her other neighbor. With enormous apprehension, I turn around to face Trifocals; he's waiting for my attempt at free verse with restrained disdain. When he proudly hands me his own sheet of paper, I find myself face-to-face with my most intimate fears: in less than half a minute, Trifocals wrote a very moving Petrarchan sonnet with matching octave and sestet. His gaze detached but his smile polite, Trifocals hands me back my poem after reading it as the crow flies. When the teacher picks up her briefcase, it's past noon. Stopping in the doorway for a moment, she looks us over:

"See you next week!" she says in a joyous voice.

Good grief.

2

I can't help it. When people ask me what I do, exactly, at the Community Center, I say "I work at pretending to work". Because that's it. There's no work to speak of; no chores, no duties, no errands. There's absolutely nothing to do at the Community Center. All day long I sit in a glass-panelled cubicle that looks like a big aquarium, poised and ready to give out information on activities organized by the Recreation Department. The phone rings about five times a day; three times out of five it's a wrong number or, if I'm lucky, a silent call. Sometimes I chat with John Frank (J.F.), the gym supervisor who has nothing to do either. I usually end up loitering in the hall or trying to corrupt the vending machine.

I've been here, drawing a salary from the City, for two years. Whenever I can, I bring over my schoolbooks and make an effort to study, but that's not always possible. Even though there's no work proper at the Community Center, interruptions abound. Teenagers who want to borrow tennis balls but have no money for the deposit. Dancers who swear they booked the reception hall weeks ago and show up ready for a hoedown. A disgruntled coach who insists on finding a box of hockey pucks he lost here last year. A father of four who refuses to accept that his kids' judo class has been cancelled. A volunteer who says he'll just "borrow" some loose change from our petty cash. To quote J.F., "Same old, same old." He's good at putting things in perspective like that.

From bitter experience, I've found that our citizens are all generally nice people until things don't go their way, which often happens. That's when they change their tune. As case in point: the junior football Coach. For the past two years, I've been dutifully catering to his needs, helping him out whenever possible and politely laughing at his jokes. Tonight however, as soon as he enters the Community Center, things go wrong. We're in September, it's raining cats and dogs outside. The Coach shows up with his whole football team in tow, this in itself an ominous sign. From my aquarium, I can already see him beckoning me over; he wants me to meet him out in the hall. I comply, a little intimidated by the forty-some players behind him, all as wide as tall. The Coach tells me they can't practice outside, because of the rain. I almost ask him why he didn't cancel his practice since it's been raining for two days straight and the football field is unusable anyway, but instead I wait while he sugar-coats his plea again:

"I know you're a nice girl. I know you can appreciate our situation here: the pitch is just too slippery for my guys."

With a large, all-embracing gesture, he shows me his team: the whole group is dripping wet, crusted over with mud, uncomfortably wriggling in soaked uniforms, reeking from sweat within a twenty-foot radius. Fifteen with a good headwind. The Coach takes me to one side. He smooths down the few hairs still clinging to his clammy forehead.

"Listen... I know the skating rink is closed, there's no ice on. My guys could practice in there. I know it's not being used for anything. I mean, it's just a waste of space.  It would be nice of you to just, you know, unlock the door…”

He's right: the indoor skating rink *is* closed.  This week, the blue-collars removed the ice to clean the concrete surface and paint the boards again.  I look at the Coach.  Just as I feared: he's serious.  He's standing there, showing off his paternal goodwill while I hesitate and the players itch with impatience.  It almost grieves me to disappoint them all, but the Coach's idea of an indoor practice is impractical.  Mentally, I enumerate why:

a) As I mentioned before, the floor's made of concrete.  A football pile-up on that kind of surface is bound to lead to some serious injuries, even with padding in strategic places.

b) Last year, the City invested thousands of dollars to retrofit the ceiling light fixtures.  One joyful kickoff could blow those things clean off the map, landing the bill right in my lap for aiding and abetting intruders.

c) An easy, linear equation: forty football players = eighty cleats = two tons of mud = beyond-filthy post-practice floor = cleaning incumbent upon the employee on duty = I = no thanks.

Just by looking at me, the Coach can tell I'm processing the reasons why I'll turn him down.  All sweetness, he puts a hand on my shoulder and leans in, plunging his rapacious gaze into mine.  One of his eyes is squinting.

“So?  What say you?  I think it's a great idea!  We won't even bother you, we'll be quiet, careful and everything. Just, you know, unlock the door so we can get in."

I can feel the whole team eyeballing me now. The keys to the skating rink burn in my hand. I understand the great human drama unfolding here. I do. If I say no, people will have wasted irreplaceable hours of their lives. Mentally, I enumerate how:

a) Forty frisky young men will have huffed and puffed just to get here, hitching a lift from busy parents or taking that once-in-an-hour bus I was talking about.

b) The same said young men will have struggled to put on the many parts of their equipment, including shoulder, elbow and knee pads, neck rolls, helmets, gloves and the aforementioned cleats.

c) The Coach will have been stuck in the backlog of traffic out from downtown, showing up panting and wheezing and fifteen minutes late, with his team already stewing in their uniforms.

d) The whole group will have toiled and strained taking out the nets from the storage lockers of the third bunker…

e) …to get their gear and equipment outside, three hundred meters down the field.

All for nothing. Sad and hard as it is, when all's said and done, I know further hesitation is pointless. But while the Coach is still trying to win me over, I suddenly notice something. A detail. Way in the back, one of the players moves. In fact, he moves two things: his head, which he motions in my direction with a knowing smile, and one of his hands, which he uses to grab his crotch. As he does this, he says something mean about me to his teammates.  I don't hear what the comment is, exactly, because the Coach is still bleating in full-lament, but I get the general idea.  That's what, finally, sways me.

"I'm sorry, but I can't help you.  Sorry."

Maybe I should've been more expansive, more illustrative, maybe I should've used extra-sweet words to justify myself.  But there's no time.  Immediately after sentence is passed, I run the gauntlet of vocal shelling from forty very angry young men.

"Just open the freakin' door!"

"What the hell's she waiting for?"

"Did you see her ugly shoes?"

Very pleasant.  While I sigh wearily and let the general outcry come to a climax, I get a vengeful fist-shake from the Coach:

"If that's how it's gonna be, I'll go and find your boss when he gets here!  You'll regret it, I can promise you that!"

Mentally, I tell him to fuck off.  Outwardly, I tell him "I see, sir", and quietly row back to my aquarium. Since all municipal offices are closed, since this is Friday night, and since I'm the only one on duty besides J.F., I know the Coach's complaint will marinate for another three days before getting anywhere.  I tell myself he'll simmer down in the interim.  For now, only one course of action remains: smiling as politely as possible, shutting the door and making my escape through the staff-only stairwell.  Turns out, my glass tank is poor protection against verbal abuse.

I dash downstairs to the gym, to blow off steam. J.F. listens to me while he's mopping the floor.  He thinks

I'm exaggerating.  In the future, he would also like to be forewarned about any upsurge of hormones in my cycle.

"Anyway, you always worry too much about things, Laurie."

He conscientiously mops the floor again, then adds philosophically:

"The Coach's just stupid."

Before he can deepen that thought, we're interrupted by an electronic bugle call: that's J.F.'s phone ringing.  With a virtuoso flick of the wrist, he answers with a curt "Yah?"  Always very brief and concise, J.F. is an expert in long-distance communications; he's constantly busy returning a call or getting a call-back, checking his messages or leaving his coordinates.  Working with him is like becoming his personal secretary, a reluctant assistant that sorts out, notes and dispatches any and all voicemails that spill out of his cell and flood the Community Center switchboard.  Seen from the outside, J.F. is totally above suspicion: tall and muscular, clean cut and perfumed, the man is Barbie's Ken incarnate, a guy who looks polished, chromed and sun-peeled to perfection, with surfboard and convertible sold separately.  The truth is that J.F. is the height of misrepresentation; he's the exact opposite of that carefully-groomed image.  His most vigorous sport is pot-smoking while his mind purrs languidly off-channel.  Never in a hurry, always late, he'll rise out of oblivion only occasionally, mostly to wheel and deal anything from stolen watches to cheap cologne.  Looking at his plastic physique, no one would ever suspect him of any wrongdoing.  And he *has* his qualities.  In fact, when it comes to finding ways of avoiding work, J.F. has proven himself quite inventive indeed.  Last summer, he spent countless hours mapping out the ideal proportions of a chips-pretzels-nachos cocktail, with all principal ingredients commandeered straight from the Community Center snack-bar. Our boss, Giles, thinks J.F. and I are his two most proficient, most faithful employees. He likes us so much, it's guilt-inducing.

J.F. hangs up quickly, as usual. He picks up his mop again, his bucket, and the thread of our conversation.

"You wanna know what your problem is, Laurie?"

"No but tell me anyway."

"Well, one of your problems is that you don't take your mind off things enough."

I look at him. He gives me the same polite smile I gave the Coach.

"When was the last time you went out and had a cold one?"

"It's been a while."

"You see!"

"Yeah, but I'm not like you. Going out for a beer won't solve my problems."

J.F. acts offended:

"It doesn't solve my problems either, but it's a start."

"A start for what? My life's stuck in neutral."

"That's because you don't have a boyfriend."

I stare at him, exposed suddenly.

"What's that got to do with anything?"

J.F. looks at his mop, a reversible type of wisdom sprawled across his face.

"Tell me the truth: how long has it been?"

I pout noticeably, in spite of myself. Difficult subject, which I don't want to broach. I try to be evasive:

"I don't really know… I don't remember."

"Come on."

"Two years."

J.F. looks satisfied.

"You see.  That's your problem: you're all alone with no one."

"I don't really mind it that much…"

"Don't give me that.  I'm sure you get bored sometimes."

"Yes, but I've been bored when I was in a couple, too.  So, this has nothing to do with that."

J.F. smiles, suddenly suspicious.  When he speaks again he blushes, eyes plunging into his bucket.

"Has it also been two years since…"

His embarrassment gives me an edge.  I know where he's driving at.  It's almost too easy.  I could take advantage of his reservations and evade again, but instead I finish his sentence:

"…since I've slept with somebody, you mean?"

J.F. glances at me, happy to be relieved from the burden of his question but still curious as to how I'll answer.

"Yes, it's been two years."

J.F. looks heavenwards, his shoulders falling from the obvious:

"My God!  Laurie, stop looking!  That's the problem!"

"Right."

"I'm telling you!  Anyone would go crazy living like a monk all the time.  There's nothing like a good ride to get back on track."

His enthusiasm gaining on me, I hesitate.  He goes on:

"Take me, for example: I've never been without it for more than two weeks."

"Is that right?"

"You bet!  Now, with Eve, my girlfriend, everything's running smoothly because she's got a good sexual appetite.  We do it all over the place: in the shower, against a wall, in my parents' basement, in my car, in her car…"

"Yeah but I've done all that already.  I need more than exotic locations to get me going.  No.  The problem is not just celibacy, it's something else."

"What then?"

"I don't know.  Things are never just right, you know? Either bad things happen or nothing happens.  And now my last session just started and already I've got a ton of presentations – well, I mean I only have one, but still.  It's making me sick.  Look at my hands."

I hold out my hands, palms facing down.  J.F. inches forward, apprehensive.

"Do you see all those red spots?  I think I'm actually developing eczema."

J.F. backs away.  He looks me over.

"Okay, see now, Laurie: I'll give you a little piece of advice.  When everything's going wrong, when life becomes a headache, tell yourself "Yeah, so what?""

""Yeah, so what?" What's that?"

"That's my secret for living life to the fullest. Instead of thinking about things to death, let it all go and tell yourself "Yeah, so what?"  It really works."

"That does sound effective…"

J.F.'s expression turns sullen as his interest suddenly switches course.  He picks up a 5-pound dumbbell and puts it back on the gym support rack.

"Look at that!  I made all those nice posters like Giles wanted, telling people to "Please put your weights back on the rack", and look at that!  The whole place's a mess. Hey, look!  One guy even spat on my poster!"

I follow J.F.'s gaze: the defiled poster glistens in the light, spit trickling down its edge.

"People just wreck everything and never respect anything."

This unusual but intense flash of frustration is cut short by another bugle call.  Sucked into his phone again, J.F. vanishes, taking with him his mop and bucket. Looking at him leave, I notice the clock on the wall.  Our shift is over: we've stopped getting paid ten minutes ago. I go back upstairs.  And there, waiting for me in the hall, is a wall-to-wall two-ton pile of mud.  I hesitate for a moment: should I clean it up or leave it to the night janitor? After due consideration, I decide to leave it to him.  While I'm busy getting my things from the glass-panelled office, J.F. comes up to punch out.

"God, it's even dirtier in here than downstairs! That's your footballers' doing, is it?"

I nod yes, and feel bad for the night janitor.  With a heavy sigh, I resign myself.

"J.F.?  Will you help me clean this up?"

We work together in silence for the next twenty minutes, clearing away the bulk of the mud.

3

Like a lot of people, I was born in Montreal, in St. Luc's Hospital, on the corner of René-Lévesque and St. Denis. I'm an only child. My mother's a social worker, my father a businessman. My mother's father was Italian, my father's mother's father was Irish, two of my great-grand-mothers were Native Americans, one was Algonquian, the other Iroquoian, my grand-father on my father's side was always proud of his Scottish origins and his wife, my grand-mother, swears that great men like Wilfrid Laurier and Louis-Joseph Papineau have ancestors that are our ancestors. That's about it. I've had a superb childhood, with no lasting memories, which again proves how pleasant it was. When I was young, our family lived near Sherbrooke street, very east. We moved to the other end of the Island of Montreal, in the West Island, when I was three. It was there, in kindergarten, that I met the all-time greatest best friend of a lifetime, also known as Veronica – or Nicky.

Ever since I can remember, Nicky always had long hair. I mean bottom-level long. She's like Samson, all her strength comes from her mane. Nicky and her hair. My take on it is that it acts as a capillary shield against the world, a sort of curtain behind which Nicky hides the scenery of her face whenever she wants peace. Our meeting was the simplest thing; it happened while we were playing elastics in the schoolyard ("'Want to be my friend?" "Okay".). A couple of years later, the powers that be decided our school should have one of those "enriched" programs for clever kids. We were both selected. Right up until the end of high school, we macerated from one such class to the next, from the Advanced Group to the Excellence Group through the rare ordeal of the Letters and Mathematics Program, where we even had to learn Latin.

Somewhere in there, during those high school years, everything changed for me. For a start, I made new friends; Nicky and I lost track of each other, as we both investigated other camps. Back home, there were also new developments: my grand-mother, who suffered from Alzheimer's, and my grand-father, who had cancer, came to live with us. My dog Buddy died and my father left us to go live with another woman. In less than a year, life completely tipped over. Predictably, I started to smoke, drink, take dope and fall vaguely in love with very little success. I also started liking school a lot less, and achieved much less academically as a consequence. Then, at fourteen, it happened: I was struck down by two very powerful, long-lasting, love-at-first-sights: the first time, with a tall blond guy who was not interested, the second time, with a tall brunette guy who was not interested either. Still, I held out hope. I loved like I lived; at full tilt but from the margins. For two years, I battled a constant flow of tormented thoughts and more suicidal thoughts. I don't know how I would've been able to handle it all if, at sixteen, I hadn't met up with Nicky again. There she was, buried alive, like me, in our school's Excellence Group. That's when we really bonded.

I'm sure now that our alliance re-formed not only because we both shared that sense of being acutely out of place, but also because the bases of our friendship were there still, still intact, even after all those lost years. Now that we were together again, we spent many a night talking, asking ourselves if living was always that tough, listening to each other's pain, opening up for the first time and ranking up countless beer bottles and cigarettes in the process, beginning to like life again instead of loathing it all. Re-finding Nicky was like rediscovering myself, although I know how clichéd it sounds when it's said like that. Anyway, over time, things, slowly, began to take an upturn. Exit all the dope, begone cigarettes, booze and hangovers – welcome exercise, healthy foods and all things outdoors. Nicky gave me a new sense of purpose because she was an interest in my life that brought on other interests. She knows everything about me, and the reverse is probably true also; she precedes or follows me everywhere, and I love her because, simply put, she's one of the greatest people on the planet.

In the caf today, just before my first Dramatic Writing class, I had lunch with her. The university cafeteria is beautiful. I like to just sit here instead of going to class. When the sun is out, the skylights pour ray upon ray of shimmering light on the varnished tables, and healthy green plants spread their glossy leaves in every corner, making even the food on our trays look fresh.

Today, on arrival, I immediately spot Nicky seated at her usual table, the one in the back, way back at the far-end of the caf. With her big boots propped up on the chair facing her, she's sitting with her face bent over her plate, half-hidden by her long hair. As I make my way over, she looks up, sees me, and makes big "come over quickly" hand gestures. The same mischievous grin she had in kindergarten illuminates her features. Her enthusiasm, however, clearly exceeds the habitual dose – something else must be going on.  Instead of saying "Hi", I dive in:

"What is it?"

"Maude called me yesterday."

Forced landing.  As I take the seat opposite her, Nicky watches as a wave of surprise sweeps through me. With a laugh, she closes the book she was reading and tucks it into her knapsack.  Still speechless, I travel back to our high school days.  Back then, Nicky held great appeal for Maude, a girl whose poor face was riddled with acne on fire.  In the beginning, Nicky resisted Maude's advances mostly because of her undeniable love of men, but after a long bout of celibacy, just before graduation, she finally gave in: she let herself be seduced by Maude and her best friend, Cedric.  One night and a threesome.

Cedric.  He's been, for Nicky, that man of many dreams, inaccessible and devouring, the one that haunts us all.  Like Nicky herself, Cedric comes equipped with a thick mop of hair that stands between him and the world like a seal of impenetrability.  The threesome happened one night when Nicky let Maude accompany her back on foot from school; on the way, they met Cedric, who was conveniently coming out of the convenience store. Immediately overwhelmed by the man's musky beauty, Nicky played it cool while the other two talked animatedly about unimportant things.  Cedric offered the girls a ride home, *his* home that is, where they could watch a movie together, he said.  Once there, all Nicky saw of the movie was the first two minutes: somewhere between the previews and the opening credits, hands started to roam free.  Nicky, by now obsessed by the thought of getting laid by Cedric, resigned herself to take on Maude as well, by force of circumstance.  I guess four hands, two tongues, not to mention other unmentionables, will sway anybody. When it was all over, Nicky never heard from Cedric again, although she wanted him now with a passion made anew by experience.  As for Maude, she plagued Nicky with phone calls and letters, pestering her from all angles, trying to make her her girlfriend.  All in awkwardness and in vain.

Now, with her piercing eyes upon me, Nicky smiles sardonically.  Having recovered from the news, I ask:

"Maude?  What does she want?"

"Can't you guess?"

I'm afraid to guess what I know.  I'm afraid Nicky will tell me that Maude still wants her.  That even after their ill-fated affair, after all the mutual blame and recriminations, all that crazy two-way bad-mouthing, Maude still wants them to make a go of it. Nicky answers:

"She still wants to be with me."

Oh God.

"Oh God."

"Yes.  She still doesn't get it.  Even after all this time, she still wants us to be a couple."

"What did you tell her?"

"Another guess, Laurie?"

I smile.

"Ah… You told her no."

"Oh no, that's putting it too mildly.  This time, I really gave her a piece of my mind, so there's absolutely no chance for a relapse."

Judging from Nicky's no-nonsense frown, Maude must've descended into Hades again.

"I hope you weren't too hard on her…"

"Listen. That one, single, lone one-night-stand was *years* ago. Eons. I don't know how to get rid of her. I told her I wasn't interested a trillion million times. I told her nicely, I told her seriously, I told her and cried, I told her and screamed, I told her with a complete arsenal of arguments – but she *still* doesn't get it. What am I supposed to do? "

Nicky draws on her grape juice. She looks at me over the straw, her face steeled by complete and utter resolve. While I take my coat off, she puts down her juice box with a sharpness that filters through her voice:

"And that's not all…"

"There's more?"

"Oh, yes. Maude wants all of us to go to the beer bash together, back at my old college."

Every year, to kick off the start of a new trimester, Nicky's former alma mater throws a beer bash, a wild anything-goes party. Even though we've been university students for a while now, Nicky and I still make it a point to attend the bashes. They're so much fun. From past involvement, I know recuperating from a bash takes a minimum of two, maybe three days. The atmosphere there is always heavy with probable erotic hook-ups and more improbable full-out sexual encounters. In other words: more sex, dope and booze again, but this time just for old time's sake.

I instantly tense on my chair, thinking about it – that, and something else. Something that was left hanging in Nicky's last sentence.

"What do you mean, Maude wants *all of us* to go to a beer bash. Who's "us"?"

"You know, the old gang. But I'm not going."

"Ah…"

I act as normally as I can but my heart thumps at a quickened pace. The old gang. I'm thrown back to high school again: one day, out of the blue, our girl-group was propelled against a new element: a boy-group. Maude, who knew Lawrence, made the introductions. Five guys, all softcore delinquents who needed a little estrogen in their ranks: Lawrence (Larry), Miguel, Guss, Yohan and Gamache. We stuck together, all of us, long enough to develop bad friendships and even worse love affairs. That phase lasted about two years. Then, some of us pursued academics, others got on the job market, and we disbanded.

What worries me now, thinking about seeing everybody again, is this: meeting old company means facing unresolved issues. For me, that's Larry. The first time I saw him, he strolled on the campus between Maude and Miguel, acting cool. I noticed him right away because he was wearing a multicolored rastacap that made Nicky piss herself laughing. Larry was not good-looking, not by a long shot. There was a no-future air about him, a wavering kind of dejection that made him look like he was destined for a long string of dead-end jobs; at sixteen, he had already given up any sense of ambition. He was sensitive, though, and dream-prone, with enough charm in his manners to make up for his indifferent stance on life and things in general. He would often just sit there, silent and placid, too uncomfortable and within himself to leave himself but too wound up to fully explore his own feelings, or anyone else's. He did a lot of dope, which earned him some sort of tacit respect from the others. When I first met him, I felt a weird sense of dread, with a sort of stupid little certainty woven around it: I knew right away something would happen between us. Nothing did. I misread the whole vibe. I soon realized I was incapable of connecting with Larry, or even simply of talking to him beyond the usual platitudes. He was, and remained, a complete mystery to me – and that made me want him, and resent him.

Nicky's still looking at me. Since I'm not talking, she focuses on trying to cut into the roast beef that lingers on her plate. Every week, she eats the same roast beef/potatoes combo, reheating the thing endlessly in the caf microwave. Every time, the meat hardens like shoe leather. I look on as she masticates with determination. In my own plate, in the tray I brought over, Today's Special of macaroni and other substances stares me right in the face with its congealed sauce and vegetables. I don't want to think about Larry anymore. I push the tray aside.

"So? What else?"

Nicky struggles to swallow another mouthful before she answers:

"There's one good piece of news."

"Yeah? What's that?"

"I'm all set to do my training course at that preschool where my aunt teaches."

For three years now, Nicky has battled depression and fatigue brought on by her zeal to rope in a bachelor's degree in Education. So this is, really, a good piece of news. I'm already jealous.

"Ah, you're so lucky! Everything always comes to you on a silver platter!"

Nicky smiles languidly.

"That's true – but hey, I've been working really hard, trying to get that diploma."

Point made.

"You're so lucky."

"You're close to the finish, too, so…"

"Yes.  But I don't know what kind of work I can get…"

"Bah, you still have three months to go before you have to figure that one out."

I nod, heaving a very heavy sigh.

"I'm sure I won't find anything.  For you, it's different.  You've been trained for something specific. You'll be a teacher.  Period.  It's so simple, so precise.  I envy that.  All I got out of Literature was general information.  I can't do anything with that.  I read a lot, I write a little.  That's it.  What will I tell people who interview me?"

Nicky concedes the point:

"It does looks bleak…"

"I don't want to work at the Community Center forever.  Or find another job flipping hamburgers all day."

"Lean meat for lean times…"

Nicky smiles at me, still gnawing:

"You know, you could go to the student placement center.  It's in the next building.  Maybe they can help you…"

I perk up.

"The student placement center?  I hadn't thought of that!  You're right!"

Nicky smiles again, again pumping away on her juice box.

"Thank God I'm here."

We both chuckle for a moment, then I force myself to eat the curdled macaroni.

**4**

My Wednesday class is a false class.  On the registration form the university sent us before the new trimester, one title attracted my attention: "Dramatic Writing".  I was intrigued, so I signed up, already thinking big thoughts about Aeschylus, Sophocles and Aristophanes – but it wasn't meant to be.  No, as incredible as it sounds, there is no class.  In its place, there's a three-hour monotone monologue by a quasi-professor who's yet unable to make the distinction between something interesting and himself; another fine example of someone who chose teaching after a misdiagnosed vocation.  Between two side-yawns, he tells us he's a "professional playwright".  I don't know if that's true or not.  He's been reading us his plays, or his essays on his plays, every chance he gets.  The only thing he's been professional at, so far, lies in the art of believing himself to be high above little us, his students.  Preaching from the pulpit, he looks down on his flock like he's delaying his own mortality in a last, selfless act of humanitarianism.  Never leaving his big chair, not even to come down to our level, he struts on wheels from one end of his desk to the other, listening intently to himself.  I've noticed how all his movements, especially those he tries to hide, are imbued with that self-love he pretends he doesn't have.  I even saw him once surreptitiously catching his own profile, reflected back to him by the glass-panelled door; chin up, chest out, he glanced at his own image with a smile, full of that blind faith he has in himself.  Last week, I spent the whole class counting the many colorful motifs on his sweater-vest. This week, as he's wearing the same sweater-vest, I migrate to thoughts about Larry.

The last time I laid eyes on him was, coincidentally, at a beer bash. That's also when problems between us got serious. Serious in a very unpleasant way. The night itself had started off fine. Just getting there, I felt so ready, totally primed, free in a great anything-goes type of mood. Once in, I toked too much, the music was too loud and the whole place buzzed with too many people: everything was just right. In spite of my overindulgences however, my memory of that night is perfectly intact.

Curtain up on the said beer bash:

Six hours into the bacchanalia and half of our gang is over and out; too drunk, too high or both, wasted beyond recognition. Only four of us make it to the end: Nicky, Maude, Larry and me. Still going strong, Nicky takes to the dance-floor, followed closely by Maude who desperately tries to close the space between them. Larry and I stay behind, drinking on, now alone at our table. Even in this setting, with music blaring and colored lights slashing through the air, Larry still looks ordinary. Even here, he's light-beige. Visible nowhere, forgettable everywhere, dissolving anywhere, he looks at me now with his small, deep-set eyes. They're strangely alight tonight. I saw him earlier on, studying me with hesitation, like something bordering on a naïve kind of probing. I sat there, saying nothing. As I sit here, saying nothing again, Larry's long body stretches; I can feel him extending his slender legs under the table. He's wearing blue pants, tight in the hips, loose on the ankles, which make him look even more lethargic. Over this, he wears a dilated T-shirt, gray, tired.  It ripples on his thighs.  Larry seems happy, his face resting serenely in the palm of his hand.  He leans in to speak to me:

"I'm glad we're together tonight."

"Really?"

"Yes.  Sometimes, when the whole gang tags along, it ruins the mood."

His decisive tone surprises me.  He's also looking at me fixedly, the deep of his eye almost hard; that's strange.

"Why do you say that, Larry?"

"You know how it is.  Gamache bosses people around, Miguel gets grumpy, Guss constipates…"

I laugh at the thought:

"That's true."

"I'm glad it's just us."

Just us.  Does he mean just us four, with Nicky and Maude, or just him and me?  He smiles and leans in again, getting closer.  I go numb, intimidated by the intimacy that inches between us.

"Ah, Laurie…  If you only knew…  Sometimes, when I'm lying in my waterbed, I think…"

I interrupt him at once.

"Ah?  You've got a waterbed?"

I prefer understatements and innuendos.  I pretend I don't care what he's thinking when he's lying in his waterbed.  I pull my whole body back from the conversation:

"I didn't know those still existed, Larry."

"They do.  Ever tried?"

"Tried what?"

I know it's a pathetic ploy on my part, but I can't answer the question directly.  It's so much on the nose, it's embarrassing.  Instead, I make as if I'm distracted by a waiter-guy picking up our empty glasses.  Larry repeats and clarifies:

"Ever slept in a waterbed before?"

Again.  That's too obvious.  I don't like that.  God. I like subtlety.  I like underplay.  Trying to remain impassive, I struggle to hide my growing irritation.

"No, I've never done that."

"You're invited then."

I busy myself emptying my last glass of beer, pretending I didn't hear properly over all that loud music. Now that he's on a roll, Larry keeps on going on:

"What's your type of guy?"

"My type of guy?"

"Yeah…"

"In one of my classes, there's a Mark.  Tall, long hair…"

I start describing Mark, a guy I have no real interest in but with whom I share a Semiotic course, once a week. I talk about him in great detail, from every perspective, just to sprinkle a little jealousy, barely a pinch, in the atmosphere.  I succeed beyond my wildest dreams because Larry's features cloud over.  He looks so utterly disenchanted, I feel forced to say, after my tirade:

"But don't worry, Larry, I always thought you had the nicest shoulders…"

I laugh for good measure, so he can't be sure whether I'm being honest or just kidding.  He also laughs, in kin, while I glance over to the dance-floor.  I quickly catch a glimpse of Nicky's long hair, twirling in the crowd.

I'd like to dance too.  I get up and leave, but Larry keeps up the pace; he won't let me distance him.  The whole night while I'm dancing, he's right there dancing next to me, in front of me, behind me...  Then, around 1:15 a.m., he and Maude get thrown out after they come to blows with two guys who were trying to steal our beers.  Nicky and I have no choice but to follow suit.

We all double back to the West Island.  I drive the four of us there; I'm still below my own personal booze/dope limit, although probably only slightly.  Nicky's in the passenger seat, angry at Maude who's busy chain-smoking reefers in the back with Larry.  Too stoned to know when to stop talking, Maude's blathering all over the place, only further exacerbating Nicky's boiling-point exasperation.  On her request, I drive Nicky home first, then head back east to drop off Maude and Larry at his place.

The apartment block where he lives is unprepossessing; brown brick walls intersect with other brown brick walls.  A few concrete-gray balconies light up the edifice, a truncated structure that looks twice too wide for its height.  While Larry fumbles for his keys in his coat pocket, I get out of the car to help Maude.  I'm trying to get her on her feet, when suddenly and without warning, she bends at the waist.

"Oh man… I'm gonna spew…"

Larry turns to her, his face without compassion.

"Maude, I don't want you up at my place if you're gonna barf again.  The last time you did that, I ended up picking up your vomit, remember?  I'm not doing that again.  If you're not feeling well, go home."

Guiltily, I catch myself hoping Maude will throw up, geyser-like, and beat a hasty retreat. She lives right down the next street, she could go home on foot, eyes closed. That would leave Larry and me alone, up in his apartment.

Like a lightning bolt straight out of destiny, my wish is granted: pausing for a moment at the ready, Maude inhales deeply, then starts to inundate the sidewalk with the last seven beers she consumed. I feel so horrible. Racked with remorse, I gently stroke her back while she's retching in gut-wrenching spasms. Larry's angry.

"Fucking shit, Maude! You can't hold your dope, you're always spewing off. You'll just have to go home. I don't want you at my place like that."

Maude lets out a death-rattle kind of groan and slumps down on the ground in her puke. In full symbiotic revulsion, Larry and I both heave at the sight. Maude is practically comatose. She moans, exhausted, while her bloated belly rises on each laborious breath under her spattered shirt. Larry looks at me.

"What do we do now?"

"I don't know. We can't leave her like that."

"She has to go back home. She can walk, it's two streets over."

"I know."

Larry bends over Maude. He firmly tugs on her shoulder.

"Maude! Maude! You have to go home!"

Maude mumbles unintelligibly. Larry sighs and swears, understandably annoyed, when, against all expectations and after some colossal effort, Maude starts to pull herself up. Larry and I help her out, each hooking an arm. I watch where I put my hands and feet. Free-standing now, Maude struggles to keep an upright position, her eyes unfocused but open. Larry looks at her:

"Maude, can you go home?"

Maude burps, which destabilizes her. She loses her balance again and stumbles back, in freefall. We grab her just in time. She looks at us, eyes widened by varying gravity. Then, leaping out from our grip, she starts to walk, staggering, over to the street. Larry and I look on, worried.

"Maude, will you be all right?"

Maude gestures comically with both hands. She yells out, at top volume:

"No problemo!..."

We watch her leave. She zigzags her way down the street, taking three steps left, two steps right. Her arms sway at her side, giving her a strange simian demeanor. Soon, she rounds the corner and disappears behind a row of houses. Larry turns to me:

"I hope she'll be all right."

I nod, feeling guilty again. Larry walks over to the main entrance. I follow him there and look on, quite coolly, as he has trouble getting his key in the lock; all those reefers and beers dull his reflexes. When at last the lock unlocks, Larry turns to me:

"After you."

Inside, the building is a little more hospitable than I expected. Long running corridors are bathed in a yellowish hue, a fuzzy kind of light that stretches from one fake chandelier to the next. The place looks like a hotel. We walk slowly, in silence, all the way to a very brown elevator. When the doors close on us, I suddenly feel like

I'll run out of air. On my left, I can feel Larry pressing against me: he dances delicately. I think that's stupid. When he sees me frown, he giggles, still playful while I concentrate on breathing correctly. I focus on the panel that lights up every time we pass a floor. The elevator stops on number 9. We get out and I find air again. Larry takes out another key from his pocket, a smaller one. He opens the door to his apartment, which is diagonally opposite the elevator.

"Welcome to my humble home."

I step inside. Everything's dark. Larry shuts the door and brushes past me. I hear him flick a switch and his apartment, a small open-plan studio, instantly floods with light. The place looks fantastic! Suffused with the soft aqueous glow of a mahogany bedside lamp, the room takes on a mauve watercolor wash with darker, bluish shades in the background. Curled up next to the stucco wall on the right is a large squashy-velvety red sofa. The back wall opens on a wide patio door and a balcony that overlooks a hidden inner courtyard. From here I can see tall maple trees, their leaves quivering in the night breeze, off in the distance, behind Larry's linen curtains. On the left side of the room, there's a computer, an old television set and a stereo. Jutting off from the vestibule, the kitchen opens on a short hall, which leads to a modest bathroom. I notice how Larry's hung all his utensils on the kitchen wall. Kind of original. Facing us is the majestic waterbed, immense, all draped in supple black.

Larry takes his coat off. Leaving me there, he resolutely makes for the stereo. Soon, music fills the room and, for a moment, I worry about the neighbors. Looking at me, Larry guesses at my thoughts:

"Don't worry about that, Laurie.  The walls are all concrete, soundproof."

I offer a silent nod, trying to ignore the fact that there's a double meaning under there somewhere.  Larry comes up to me but abruptly branches off to the kitchen, where he disappears:

"Would you like something to eat or drink?"

I'm still wearing my coat.  I take a step forward, hesitant; somehow, I feel really nervous now.  Out of nowhere my heart's beating so fast, I think I might faint. How ridiculous.  I just have to get a grip on myself, that's all.  I try to speak in a casual, clear voice:

"Yes.  I'd like a glass of water, please."

Larry comes out of the kitchen, smiling.

"A glass of water?  Girls are all the same.  They all want a glass of water."

Larry disappears again, back into the kitchen.  I wonder how many girls came up here asking for a glass of water.  I feel so stupid.  I'd like to leave.  I'd like to run back to my car and peel off.

I get rid of my coat and sit on the floor facing the bed.  Larry comes out of the kitchen carrying a beer for himself and a glass of water for me.  He hands me the glass, which I take; I can see water frothing in there, in little white particles.

"Thanks."

"You're welcome."

Larry opens his beer.  The "pchitt!" almost makes me jump out of my skin.  I'm so tense, my God.  And how can he still drink?  Yuck.  While I look on nauseously, Larry sits on the edge of the bed in front of me:

"Did you see how Maude was trying to get it on with Nicky? Again? She's desperate. Poor Maude."

"Poor Nicky."

"That's right. Poor Nicky. I guess she's getting pissed off."

"Getting there, yes."

"Speaking as a guy, I must say though, I understand what Maude's going through."

I frown involuntarily:

"How do you mean?"

"I mean, as a guy, I know how Maude feels. It's tough to be alone all the time."

"You know this as a guy? I see."

"I just mean I've been alone a lot, you know."

"Yes. You've always been single, I think, ever since I've known you…"

Larry looks at me, a little taken aback. He shrugs and takes an indolent tone:

"Yeah but I've had a lot of one-nights, you know…"

I frown again, this time on purpose. I've never heard or seen anything that gives any semblance of credence to this statement. As far back as I can remember, Larry never had a girlfriend, or a lover. Feeling his unease, I look at him less. While I fiddle about with some loose strands poking out of the carpet, he presses on:

"It's just that… It's not easy to always be on the look-out for someone. Over time, it gets boring to always wonder about that dream-girl. Where is she? What's she up to?"

My heart's racing like crazy again.  When I dare to look up, Larry's looking down at the carpet I'm no longer playing with.  He's smiling to himself, lost in his thoughts:

"You never know, Laurie.  You never know how things can turn out…"

He said that with complete apathy.  Throwing his head back, he downs his beer in one go.  Over the neck of the bottle, his eyes meet mine.  Oh no.  There's no place for me to hide, nothing to cover my tracks with, no way to loop the moment.  No time either.  I plunge and ask:

"How am I supposed to hear this?"

Larry looks at me, full on now, and in that split-second, we both know we know.  It's the end of all pretences, and the beginning of acute discomfort.  There's nothing else in the world but this moment, terrible and without refuge, where reaction tilts on the edge of real action.  He says, unenthusiastically:

"Are you sure you don't want a beer?"

"I'm sure."

"I think I want you."

Did I hear him right?  Fortunately, he continues:

"I mean tonight, you were talking, I was listening and it just clicked, you know?"

"It clicked?"

"Yes."

I look away, way over to the patio door, to give myself some latitude, some protective indifference.  When something has been out of reach for years, when you've thought about it before going to bed, and in bed, when you've daydreamed the hell out of all intents and purposes, investigated all available options, telling yourself "God, if only…", you never really believe it can happen.  You've invented and imagined everything because you're convinced you'll never get to experience any of it in the heat of actual life, in real time, because you know it's all make-belief – and there's a limit to handing yourself over to your romanticism, however corny or genuine it might be.

I can't find an answer. Larry fixes his eyes on me like he's drowning in slow-motion. A long pause, until finally I come up with the first dumb thing that comes to mind:

"What do you mean, exactly?"

I know, I know. It's a poor attempt at flipping the situation around, but it's also a safety net: I want to make sure I'm not imagining, misconstruing or blindly hallucinating things here. Larry looks at me in agony. He lets himself slide on the floor next to me and starts to tear at the label on his beer bottle.

"I wanna be with you, you know… *"with"*…"

His emphasis. I keep my eyes down but I know he's looking at me head-on now. I'm so terrified, so utterly uncomfortable, a ton of disjointed thoughts flood my psyche. I worry about inconsequential things like hair and makeup, breath quality and looking stupid. God, I'm scared. I bow my head. Before I can pick up the carpet thread I was playing with, Larry caresses my hair, gently, with unexpected tenderness. I bite my lower lip. He leans in and kisses me fully on the cheek. I still can't look at him, but I venture out a hand in his direction, to touch him on the arm. Larry tightens his embrace, slowly kissing my face everywhere, and finally it happens: my hang-ups melt one by one, all my fears wilt behind me and dissolve because I want him so much. When at last his lips close on mine, I'm ready. We kiss long, then deep. I try to keep myself lucid, to feel it all, to savour it all. His tongue pets the roof of my mouth in a quick succession of timid little laps while he takes hold of my neck, grabbing tight at the nape. His lips are still only half-parted, though; when I kiss him back, I get the impression of penetrating a young girl, and a virgin one at that. I feel like I can't let myself go, that if I do, I'll break something sacred, or come up against some immovable object....

Something's missing.

I wonder if he's hesitating because he's unsure of the extent of my desire for him. To make this absolutely clear, I slowly straddle him and take off my shirt. Under me, Larry freezes. He's still holding his beer in his right hand, and his left hand is suspended in midair, not making contact with me anymore. He lets me kiss him again, but with something like a distant stance. Meanwhile, I get my bra out of the way, in case it also intimidates him; sliding one hand backwards, I unhook the thing with one curt manoeuvre. Larry places a hand on one of my shoulders. Thinking he wants to look at me, breasts bared, I pull away but come face-to-face with his pale, vacant stare. Only now do I realize the extent of the mood-shift; Larry moves me aside and gets up. Now half-braless, I react on instinct and cover myself with my hands. I gaze up at him, disconcerted. He glances away and paces the room.

"Larry? Are you all right?"

Setting down his beer on the nightstand, Larry doesn't answer me or look in my direction. I quickly put my bra back on and look for my shirt; it landed between the bed and the sofa. I feel really strange, somewhere between a state of shock and very explicit humiliation.

Reaching over the bed, I recuperate my shirt and slide it over my head. I'm decent again, but Larry still keeps his back to me. He's facing the stereo. When he finally speaks, his voice is thin, drenched in cold evasion:

"I still have feelings for someone else, Laurie."

I stay perplexed. What's he talking about? Someone else? What does that have to do with anything? Why is he bringing this up now?

I say nothing. Silence helps Larry regain some composure. He goes on:

"It's just that I'm confused. When I think about her, I want you. When I think about you, I want her."

I find my voice again.

"Why are you telling me this now? Why didn't you say anything before?"

"I don't know… I have to sort myself out before we go any further…"

Larry comes back towards me and sits on the bed. He sighs and plunges his head in his hands, expelling that nice feeling of self-possession he had a moment ago. I watch him for a moment, then I get up and head for the kitchen. While I pour myself another glass of foggy water, he comes in and takes me in his arms, chin buried in my neck.

"I'm so sorry, Laurie. I feel really bad, but I'm confused. I'm really sorry."

I pull away. My initial surprise is mutating into a massive furious gale. I'm angry now, mostly because I feel vulnerable, exposed: I've showed him how much I wanted him and I'm angry at myself because my attraction was too obvious, too intense. I'm angry because I think he's stupid, teasing me and leading me on before letting me down with a big fat thud. Larry issues another emaciated "Sorry…", but I've had enough. I have to go. Now.

And I leave. As fast as I can. And of course he lets me; it makes it easier for him.

That's the last time we saw each other.

After that and since, I went back to my life as it was – that is, to forced celibacy, to ceaseless abstinence, to lonely popcorn-hockey nights in front of the television, with long sighs during commercials. The problem is not loneliness. The problem is constant loneliness. Solitude is a good thing; it's isolation that kills. That raw aching, of being swept over by unfulfilled desires, of having beating impulses at all levels, heart, mind and body included and excluded, and to never be able to act on any of them, is enough to finish off anybody. That's the problem.

The beer bash looming on the horizon makes this all the more obvious, painful. I know it's ridiculous, but there it is: if I stay home instead of going, I'll feel like I've condemned myself to complete and utter seclusion. I have to go. Just to make sure I don't miss out on anything. To free myself of the weight of guilt that comes from being afraid of spending all my life alone, with no anchor anywhere, no comfort, no respite, no security, caught in an endless emotional wander, a sharp little torment that cancels all will to live, throwing it in a great crude void. I hate being that desperate, but there it is.

I've since heard that Larry's story with the "other girl" didn't work out, and that he's been as chaste and celibate as I am. Hmm...

I land back on the planet. My Dramatic Writing professor is rounding off his hour-long exposé on soliloquys. He's facing us now, his features composed in a false mask of humility, describing how he directed a play in Milan, and the success it garnered there (or so he says). I try to forget Larry and listen instead to what the professor's saying:

"I know how difficult it is, for you, to understand what constitutes a masterpiece when it's impossible for me to reproduce it here, in all its theatrical splendor. That being said, I want to share my experience with you. It is essential. When you write your own play – as indeed you will, in a few weeks' time – and receive my commentaries, suggestions and guidelines, it will be easier for you to proceed and make the necessary corrections if, first and foremost, you are familiar with the extent of my experience."

I have to control myself – because I actually feel like I'm on the verge of tears. I can live with the day-to-day need for a teacher to try and impress upon us the vastness of his or her knowledge. But to be forced to write a play, and have it broken down by that idiot with his "constructive critique" (as he says again) is just too much to ask.

The beer bash is in two weeks.

5

Just out of curiosity, I went to my local job center yesterday.  There was nothing for me there, no prospects, no career, no future.  True, I still haven't looked into the university's student placement service, but I don't want to get my hopes up just yet.  Somehow I have this lingering feeling that I've wasted years of my life on school benches, waiting for breaks and recesses, reading at surface-level, taking messy notes, writing useless commentaries, biased dissertations or just poorly-drafted midterm papers that get me by anyway because the teacher's tired and no longer focused on evaluating my evaluation of Nietzsche's own evaluation of the world, or any similar concept.  I know it already: I'll graduate soon with high honors and every possible requirement for a long-lasting, endless career in job searching.

I must admit though, my school program has its high points.  For instance, my Thursday class.  This is a seminar on Rationality.  I realize taking a class on anything rational is weird on my part (Nicky convulsed with laughter when I told her, saying I'm the least rational person she knows), but I liked the idea of picking up some real hard empirical data.  Turns out, the professor's actually interesting, which is essential, and he knows his stuff, which is useful.  Today, after finishing a long theoretical sermon on Michel Foucault, he turned to face us squarely, a paternal smile forming under his expensive glasses:

"Oh yes, before I forget: I'd like to digress for a moment.  You know, I feel that my work here, as a professor, should both include *and* surpass the basics of your lesson plan. In other words, I'd like to accompany you on your academic journey as best I can. I want you to know that I'm entirely at your disposal if you have any questions regarding your career opportunities."

My God. Yes! That's it!! That's it, exactly!!! Help offered freely, brilliantly, generously. Is it even possible? God, I'm so scared. I'm scared of getting my degree, of graduating and getting that serially-numbered diploma they hand out to everybody, and then realizing I've studied, worked and slaved all this time for nothing. I'm absolutely terrified. And now here's someone who can help me, who can tell me what to do, how to go about fulfilling my destiny and living life on purpose! Yes?!? I look at the man again. He's smiling to us with that sympathetic self-confidence that just seems to ooze out of him, keeping us afloat by proxy. My God, how I envy him. He's so well-adjusted; relaxed but firm, a happy mix.

While he goes on talking, I zone out for a minute, still absorbed by his image. He's wearing loose loafers with which he treads among us, felt-like, answering questions, his ample shirt softly beating his back when he turns to write on the blackboard. I've just decided that I really like him when he suddenly turns around again and spots me. Up until now, he's been talking at large, scanning students' faces indistinctly – but now his eyes land, surprised, on my beatific expression. I immediately retreat, hating to be obvious, desperately trying to recompose my features – but he jauntily smiles back at me before continuing:

"If you feel I may be able to assist you, don't be afraid to come and meet me at my office. I'll be happy to help you out in any way I can."

Again I'm bewildered. I feel uplifted, joyous even, but underneath all that joy, somehow, I'm very calm; the terrible anguish that usually possesses me at the mere mention of the words "job market" has suddenly subsided. Evaporated and extinguished on the strength of a few kind words. Smiling to myself now, I look down at the sheets of paper on my desk, at the little poem I tried to write about Larry instead of taking notes, and I give in to that novel, tranquil notion, that maybe, just maybe, all is not lost.

Speaking of mediocre poems: thus far, and as expected, my Poetry class has yielded its fair share of painful oral performances, with several students already having done their presentations. I must say though, the teacher also knows her stuff, and her comments have been spot-on, surprisingly so. With the exception of a few tearful classroom exits, and a few more bruised egos, all's gone well. I like being in an audience while someone else reads. It gives me space to analyse. To date, I've counted four types of poetry-reading students, bearing in mind I'm generalizing here:

a) The student who doesn't want to read because he/she is too shy:

In a barely audible voice, this sacrificial victim goes through strophes and stanzas at top speed, dispatching a poem no one can hear or savour. A torture administered to the executioner by the executioner. The message? Anything this person has written, and by extension their own person, has no intrinsic merit whatsoever, nothing deserving either our time or our interest. The reception? No one cares so everybody dumps on the poem, and its author, mercilessly.

b) The student who doesn't want to read because he/she is an "artiss":

This specimen also looks like someone going up the gallows, but this poor soul likes to make a scene on the way over. Here we have to endure many sighs between each halting sentence, because, as one of them told us, "words hurt". Uh-huh. Holding the poem at a distance so as to not be blinded by his/her own genius, this author is sometimes even taken seriously by other students. Moving on.

c) The student who wants to participate because he/she actually likes this:

This model is interesting; ebullient, involved, excited – all good. Problems may surface at a later time, however, when discussing other people's poems becomes an excuse for constantly referring to one's own work. That said, if limited to reading his/her poem with sincere enthusiasm, this type of author can be most endearing.

d) The student who couldn't care less:

By far the funniest. Detached, spaced out, bored. It's funny to watch – unless the boredom's too intense. Then everybody gets infected real fast, with people venting any and all frustrations with or without any sensible relation to the poem at hand. Boredom is highly flammable in a Poetry workshop.

Of course, with my own presentation looming large, my phobia for public speaking has increased tenfold. I still have no idea what kind of poem I should write and my miserable attempts at taking inspiration from Larry have proved, so far, completely fruitless. With so much riding on so little, my poem-read-aloud is taking on a nice apocalyptic sheen, giving me many doses of cold sweats and sleepless nights. I know I'll probably get by in the end, but still. My presentation is in one week; one more week of exponentially shrinking self-confidence, conversely expanding self-doubt, and no poem.

Instead of trying to find something to kick-start my creative wheels, after class I decide to stop by my grandparents' house – my dad's parents, that is. They still live in the east end of Montreal, like us before them, in a duplex that looks like a dentist's office. When I get there, right away, Grandma welcomes me with open arms.

"Laurie! I'm so happy to see you!"

My grandmother is a strong-willed woman, resilient and hard-headed. She handles, manages and knows everything that goes on in our family. Everyone fears her with affection. As she gets older, however, her softer side steadily trickles through. Looking at me now, she ushers me in with a series of little pats on the back.

"Come inside, come inside. Grandpa'll be along soon. He just woke up from his nap."

I can hear my grandfather close a drawer behind his closed bedroom door. I can picture him now, putting on his suspenders. Grandpa's as strong as Grandma, but his strength is purely physical; in the last few years, he's had three heart attacks, two cancers (first throat, then prostate) two bypass surgeries, one tumor in the lungs, a bout of thrombosis and a long fling with angina. He turned eighty-two last month. Sure enough, when the bedroom door opens on him, there he is with his suspenders and a large smile.  Wrapping his arms around me, he gives me a tight hug.

"How are you, sweetheart?"

I love my grandparents with all my heart.  Over and above reason.  Unconditionally.  I tag along as they both head for the kitchen.  My grandmother motions for me to sit down:

"So?  How are you?"

"I'm fine, Grandma.  Just a little tired."

"How's school?"

I smile a forced smile.  Instantly, my grandparents frown together, in unison.

"It's going okay.  I guess I'm a little worried about what I'll do after graduation.  I'm worried I won't be able to find work."

Grandma leans in.

"Why wouldn't you be able to find work?  A nice intelligent girl like you!"

If only my grandmother could come along with me on all those job interviews.  She'd be convincing prospective employers left and right.  Grandpa thinks practically:

"They're training you for the job market.  They wouldn't give you all those courses if they weren't useful."

My grandmother gets a little miffed.  She glares at her husband:

"Dad!  Will you stop that!  Those courses are not useless.  She's working so hard!"

"That's what I said!  I'm sure they wouldn't teach all those things if there wasn't any work in that field."

They look at each other, agree, then turn their attention back to me.

"I guess I could become a Literature teacher or something, but I think I'd have to study some more."

"You would go for your master's, then?"

"Yes, but I don't feel like it, Grandma. I don't feel like teaching. I don't have enough patience to explain things. I don't have that sort of calling."

"What would you like to do instead?"

"I don't know. I'd like to have a job that pays well but that doesn't spill too much into my real life, you know what I mean? A job that's just a job."

My grandparents smile and laugh knowingly, nodding their heads at my great naivety. Grandpa homes in on factual matters:

"That's all very well, sweetie, but you'll still need enough to pay your bills."

"But what if I never find my true calling and end up living on welfare? I'm always thinking about what kind of job I'd like, and I can't find anything. It's like there's no path or anything for me."

My grandmother looks at me head on with those piercing blue-green eyes of hers.

"Now you listen to me, Laurie. You'll see, you don't know it yet, but things in life always fall into place. You just have to give it some time."

"What if I don't make it? What if I end up living in a box on a street corner?"

My grandparents laugh, serene. For them, this is the height of absurdity. My grandmother looks at me again. There's never any doubt in her eyes:

"You won't end up living in a box on a street! Believe me. I've seen a lot of things in my life, I've seen a lot of people trying things and falling flat on their faces. Listen to me: you'll make it."

My grandmother squints at me with utter confidence. Next to her, grandpa nods gravely. Grandma goes on:

"Your grandpa and I know it. We even told each other as much the other day: you'll succeed, you just don't know it yet."

I look at my grandparents looking at me: they both have that same air of absolute conviction, their eyes decided, categorical and proud. Full of love. I feel so warm, enveloped, I'm afraid I'll start crying, but my grandmother suddenly gets up with a little bounce:

"Oh! I forgot. You didn't see the pictures we took!"

My grandparents just got back from a vacation trip. They went to see my father. My father lives at the other end of the earth, in the States, with his new wife and their new kids. He moved there "for business", five years ago. I saw him twice since then, each time because he had to come back here "on business". Last year, I didn't get a birthday card. Or a Christmas card.

My grandmother comes back with stacks and stacks of pictures.

"You'll see how beautiful it is over there! It's like being on another planet."

Grandpa concurs:

"It's not too humid."

My grandmother opens the first pack. On the first picture, we can see a little bit of the Grand Canyon. In the foreground, there's my father kissing his wife. Grandma quickly puts away this picture, but on the next ten pictures, we can see my father with his wife standing next to their new pool, my father with his wife in their new house, my father and their kids with their new cars... The more we dig into those pictures, the more I get nauseous. My grandparents notice this, of course. Grandma puts away all the pictures. She looks at me, her face hard now, but her eyes water when she starts speaking. There's a quaver in her voice.

"Laurie, your dad misses you. He'd like you to call him more often. He'd like you to visit. You could stay with them, you wouldn't have to go to a hotel."

I stare ahead, downwards. I don't feel like answering. I don't feel like saying anything. I feel like leaving, right now, I feel like getting out of here.

"Laurie, your dad talks about you a lot. He's afraid to lose you. You two barely speak anymore."

The truth is right there, but I can't say it. Not to my grandparents. I can't tell them that every time I call my father he's busy, always busy, distracted, doing other stuff. He never listens. Or if he does, we get interrupted. I don't know how many times I've talked to him only to realize he wasn't listening to me anymore because he was talking to the kids, or to his wife in the background. I'm tired of trying to show him I'm important.

I don't want to hurt my grandparents, but I have to leave, I have to leave, I have to leave. My grandmother plows on, all in goodwill:

"You know, you should go over there, you'd like it."

"I can't do that, Grandma."

I want to die, now, God, please take me now. Grandpa, who has stayed silent for the last few minutes, tries to clear a path:

"Laurie, leave all those old stories behind. Just put some concrete on top of all that, you'll be all right."

My dear, dear grandfather, and his concrete.

"I've tried doing that, Grandpa, but weeds grow through concrete."

My grandparents laugh at the thought, but no one says anything anymore. I inhale deeply and get up.

"Well, I better get going…"

I can see them both reining in their disappointment, but they respect my decision. They understand. They kiss and hug me and I escape. When I start my car, my anxiety settles a bit, but as I get on the highway, I can't breathe properly anymore.

That's when an idea comes to me.

I should write a letter to my father.

My father's almost like a stranger to me now, I don't know him anymore. When I don't keep myself in check, when I let all the anger within me seep out, a great big sadness overtakes everything and things become unlivable really fast. It's such a dangerous, slippery slope. Bad thoughts get so clear and real when pain like that hits. I know I'm more hurt than angry. I also know that all the anger comes from feeling so hurt. So there: I'll write to him. My last attempt at making contact. Not an easy thing, but I'll be honest. I'll tell him that:

a) I miss him too
b) I still love him
c) I don't like his wife and kids

Good God.  I can't tell him that!  I know I used to tell him I loved him a hundred million times every minute of every day when I was small – but now?  It's impossible. I've never told him I loved him after he left us.  I never dared.  That was too scary.  I was scared of him leaving again, somehow, moving further away, leaving me again while I stayed behind, loving him all by myself.  It's true. Even with my little-girl love, the absolute love of childhood, the purest love of all, I couldn't keep him with us.

When I get home, I manage to write about fifteen pages.  A long letter that did me a lot of good.  I look at it now, resting in my hands.  Even if I say hard things in there, my handwriting is amazingly neat and regular.  I don't know if my father will understand.  Maybe I'm making a mistake.  Maybe I should be content with our sporadic, trivial conversations.

I look at the letter again, at its tidy pages.  I can't send it.  I'm not ready yet.  No, I'll just stick it in this drawer, here.  There.  That's it.  I mean, I know I should confront that stuff once and for all, but not now, not yet. Even though I'm tired of things left unsaid, of being in pain and not saying anything, I'm just too scared, scared of all those pent-up emotions stacking up, piling up, creating a wall between my father and me, compact and solid, impassable…  A wall made out of concrete.

6

I'm all emptied-out. After the long letter to my father, nothing else came to mind. No organised thoughts, no daydreams, nothing constructive – no poem for my Poetry workshop. Before all else fails me, I call Nicky. My desire to see Larry again is really strong. Distractingly so. I won't even pretend to fight it: I want to go to the beer bash, period. Well, not period. Semicolon, rather, because I also want to convince Nicky to come with me, to hook-up again with the old gang. I get a cold reception:

"Are you crazy?… I'm trying to avoid Maude like the plague!… Do you really think I'll go there and put myself back in her clutches?…"

"I know, but, you know, 'could be fun."

My tone is anything but persuasive – and yet Nicky still hesitates. I can tell by the way she lets each of her sentences trail off. While she takes her time thinking, I edge in a harsh comment:

"Wouldn't you like to get out of that old-lady mode we're stuck in? Don't you remember a long-lost time when we'd be in a line-up in front of a bar instead of yawning in front of the TV? We're living like hermits!"

"Speak for yourself, Laurie… I am perfectly content…"

Those ellipses again.

"Come on, Nicky. I know you're bored. So am I. We never do anything anymore!"

Nicky stays silent. I know I'm scoring points.

"Listen, you can't let your fear of Maude run things."

"Hmm… That's true."

Her tone has softened. Then it hardens again:

"Okay, you know what? You're right! Maude can go to hell! I wanna go to the party too."

"Great! You're really coming?"

"Damn right! I'm not gonna let Maude ruin my life. I'm going."

"You're sure now? You won't change your mind on me?"

"Not a chance."

I sound Nicky out again, just to make sure she's on solid ground here, but I can tell it's true: her mind is really made up. She's going, we're going! When we hang up, I'm happy. Being at a party with Nicky beats being at a party without her anytime. Still, I can't help thinking something's wrong. My stomach's upset. Apart from the obvious trepidation that comes from the prospect of seeing Larry again, what really bothers me is the feeling that maybe it's all a mistake – that maybe I should just forget the whole thing and stay home, like a good little girl in old-lady mode.

In my glass tank at the Community Center, J.F. roars out loud, confirming my worst suspicions.

"Ah, Laurie… I can see you coming from a mile away: you think Larry's gonna be there and you hope you'll get another shot at seducing him. Right?"

J.F. never met Larry in his life. Any information J.F. has on Larry comes from me. I hate the way he can just throw my own thoughts back in my face, like a mirror. His feet resting on the desk in front of me, his head tilted back on the chair he's sitting in, J.F. rocks to and fro, looking nonchalantly in my direction.  He giggles again, getting on my nerves:

"I know that's what you're thinking, I just know it."

"First of all, I've never *seduced* Larry, if you must know.  Second of all, I'm just curious about seeing him and the gang again, that's all…"

J.F. nods along with himself:

"You just wanna see if you still have a shot at him."

"Come on."

"Come on yourself, Laurie.  You can at least admit that much.  You've been alone for awhile, you're bored, there's a guy just around the corner and you want to recharge your batteries.  Perfectly normal."

"You're way off.  I don't want to be with anyone.  Being in a couple is overrated.  I'm free now, totally.  No more compromises, no more stupid pointless fights, no half-assed commitments, no in-laws, no romantic Valentine's crap, no hassles, no manoeuvering and little power games.  No, J.F., I'm at peace.  Finally at peace."

J.F. looks at me, unimpressed.

"Everything you just said is bullshit."

"Excuse me?  Why?"

"Because it's easy to say you don't need anybody when there's nobody around.  We're all strong and cool when our emotions are switched off.  But you just wait.  One guy who really sets you alight and all your nice little ideas will fly out the window."

J.F. rocks in his chair with even more impetus.

"You really think I want to get back in the couple-squabble game?"

"That's exactly what you want."

I very maturely pout and shrug. J.F. leaps up, all full of annoying energy.

"All right. I'd love to just sit here all day and listen to your stories about guys you want but don't love, but I've got to get back to the gym to make sure people are putting the weights back on the racks."

"So go."

"Bye-bye!"

J.F. leaves, his step light. As soon as he's out of sight, I dive back into my thoughts. I'm happy to be single, I really mean that. My last relationship was so terrible, it makes me wary of getting involved again, be it with Larry or anybody else.

I'd rather not think about that now. Anyway, I want to take advantage of my shift to think about my poem... Seriously, I really want to write something good, quickly done but nicely put, nothing calculated or soulless. This time, I really want to play it straight, be inspired, produce a nice piece of work, read it in front of the class, get above-average reviews, a good grade, and then get home just in time for dinner. I really want to do something worthwhile – honestly.

After work, still poem-less, I try sitting in our backyard to catch some sun and just relax. My presentation is next Tuesday. That's in four days. It's chilly outside but I stay put, taking in some much-needed fresh air like it's still a valid commodity out here in the suburbs. Slouching on a plastic garden chair, I get a sense of my surroundings: I listen to birds I can't see, breathing in the moist earth-laden air I can't see either. Hmm, that's nice, it smells like nature's falling asleep, as it does periodically, since time immemorial. I'm sure it was just the same three hundred years ago. I wonder if great Native Americans lived here before, hunter-gatherers or warriors, all living together… or maybe there was nothing here, just woods and forests, maybe the villages were farther away, maybe closer to the river: by car, the St. Lawrence is only ten minutes away. Maybe some of my aboriginal ancestors travelled through here... Oh, yes, the poem... Maybe I should write on that subject, Native Americans, or the colony... No, that's too complicated. Hmm... Maybe a poem about a legend, or a myth, like stories told by the early settlers?... Yes, but I'd have to think a lot. And do some research. Anyway, it's too much info for a poem. Leaves me cold. I wonder if people of old wrote poems. I'm sure they did. People are people, whatever the time or place. Maybe they wrote love poems. Oh, no, not a love poem, yuck. Anyway, to get anything out, I'd have to be in love to start with, so that's a joke. No, if my ancestors wrote poems, they must've been about wars, animal spirits or the land... Ha! I *should* write about the land, my land: the West Island! Ha! Ha! Dear old West Island. Subtitle: a danger-zone for those who venture here unsuspectingly. Yes! Here be dragons!

It takes me ten minutes. I write the whole thing down, here in my backyard, scribbling on a notepad on my knees, in ten minutes. When I'm done, I stretch a little, get up and tuck the notepad in my pocket. Without revising or rereading anything, I stroll around. From experience, I know that not writing is still writing. In my mind, the text is still taking shape, still forming, getting more precise, correcting itself. I just have to let it go. Just as I thought, while I'm busy pulling out dead branches from under a bush, the poem comes back to me on its own volition, requiring a little tune-up.  I take out the notepad, quickly make the correction and tuck it back in.  I inhale deeply, kneel down and bury my hands in the earth; it's cool and damp, very autumn.  I can feel a big worm moving between my fingers.  I take my hand away, a little disgusted, but I watch the worm work and weave its way for a full half-hour.  Then I get up and inhale deeply again. The sky is steel-blue, cloudless, the air is crisp, windless. I can feel the poem, still tugging at me.  I walk around for a few more minutes, then sit back down again.  I take out my notepad and read the whole thing to myself, aloud.

Okay.  It'll do.  It sounds more like a song than a poem, although maybe a song is really just a poem with music on top, I don't know.  All I know is the end could be better.  I mean, I could find something more effective if I really wanted to.  If I really wanted to.

## 7

This morning in my Rationality class, the professor gave us back our very important start-of-term papers – the corrected version, that is – on Descartes. Swooshing between rows of students in his loafers, he lets my copy, marred by a C-, fall plainly on my desk before shuffling on.

C-? That's almost a D! As a crowning statement, the professor wrote a message across my front page: "I allowed for latitude here because I know you can do better".

I can't believe it. C-! I'm so profoundly disgusted with myself that I get out of class, I get up and leave right in the middle of everything, while the professor's still talking. I don't care what he thinks or says, I'm leaving. But then, just when I think I've managed to outrun my scruples, anxiety catches up with me right there in the subway; I start feeling strange, worrying about little things. My vision gets blurry, my ears feel stuffed. I start to panic on the orange line, between Place-St-Henri and Vendôme, where the tunnel stretches over an approximately interminable distance. My God, what if I can't breathe anymore? I'll be stuck here, stuck under those big cement platforms with all those people pressing against me! Details swirl around in odd patterns while I'm convinced I'm losing my mind. I try concentrating on a shampoo add. The white letters on the poster look grotesque, somehow, like I'm not able to make sense of what I'm seeing anymore. I feel feverish, sweat's pearling on my forehead, near the hairline. I'm so dizzy, good grief, I think I'm about to faint. All around, people are chatting and talking; the noises they make stab me, making no sense, like it's all going backwards, stabbing again while everything's going too fast, getting muddled. My mind's racing but I can't think, everything's out of sequence, moving in fits and starts.

I get out of the subway at Vendôme, to catch the train back home. I climb up the steps, hanging on to the handrail to keep a grip on reality. A woman is struggling up, in front of me. The stairs are congested. I need to get out! The crowd's too dense. I want to get out! I'm nauseous, there's no air, there's too many people.

I shove the woman aside and offer some sort of apology (in my head). Then I sprint on, running off into the distance and into more stairs. After one painfully shallow intake of breath, I rush up, climbing four steps at a time. I emerge out of the subway station just as my train is divinely pulling in. Onboard, I'm immediately welcomed by the familiar rancid air; reassured, I curl up in it, still pale and trembling, huddled on a bench near the exit.

I know exactly what just happened. It's that presentation in Poetry that's plaguing me again… and now that C-, creeping in as well. I get so much stress from school, it just clots everything, every which way, at random. This time, it happened in the subway. Next time, who knows? I have to keep myself under control, I must focus on my breathing, to slow it down.

The train starts off, bringing with it the crowd that was shutting down my system, a moment ago. Back in the subway, when they were all standing pressed up against me, people made me feel stifled, suffocated. Here, sitting neatly in compartmentalized sections, people don't make me feel anything.

"Ticket!... Ticket!..."

Ticket-Ticket approaches, hunting for fares. I plunge head first into a book, hoping they'll go away, him and his mustache. Reading comforts me, it gives me a false but essential sense of security. I hate to admit it, but I know school is not solely responsible for my anxiety. It's Larry, too: I'm actually scared of seeing him again. There's this impression that sticks in my mind: I shouldn't go to the beer bash, I just shouldn't go. The idea that the whole thing could go wrong paralyzes me. What if he ignores me, what if he pretends he doesn't know me, what if he tells me to bug off in front of everybody? What if he's mean to me? It could happen. The party's in seventy-two hours. God, I have to calm myself down.

Ticket-Ticket walks past me; he's busy. Joy. I try plunging back into my book. It's not working. I've read the same sentence four times already, with no recollection of what it was about. My thoughts begin to rise again, whirling again. I get even more nauseous than before, panic galloping at me, almost within reach – when something outside myself piques my attention. It happens all of a sudden, like an excuse to stop thinking about things that worry me: my eyes hook on the bench opposite me, on the big slack testicles of a middle-aged man sitting there. Thick large testicles, well-rounded and aged, hanging loosely in the deep of his pants. The fabric, stretched, extending over the balls, betrays their density. I look on unashamedly. I'm not only eyeing the man's privates to evacuate excess stress, but also because I'm deeply curious about seeing what lurks there. I want to look at that full crotch head on, until I'm properly sated, until I've weighted their load, estimated their experience.

J.F.'s right: I need to get laid.

Perhaps because he felt x-rayed, the man with the balls lifted his head a moment ago. Perplexed, he's been looking at me looking at his groin for a few crucial seconds. In one instant, I become fully aware of my absolute lack of ethics. When our eyes meet, I blush uniformly, complete with hot-flashes and shrivelled toes. The man clears his throat, very insulted, and unfolds a newspaper lengthwise, hiding his genitals with it.

I put away my book. I'm too far gone, too far off anyway. That C- really shook my confidence. I'm sure now that my poem is also under par. I can't read that in class! I take it out of my school bag and read it again. I knew it. It's horrible! I hate the words I've chosen, words that float instead of flowing, that move along spinelessly when they should stand up resolutely against mediocrity. Fake, fake, fake, it's all fake. My poem stinks, I'll have to change it, I can't read that in class, it's a nonentity, impossible to employ, useless to exploit, a nullity that idly contemplates itself, fondling its own grammarian profile and getting off on precocious punctuation marks. Yuck.

Twice now, I've had the same nightmare: I get up to read my poem and all the students laugh at me even before I say anything. I just stand there while everybody roars. And when the teacher motions for me to start, I can't, words on the page disorganize, in full mutiny against me, forming symbols I can't recognize, and people laugh, and the teacher writes "Fail" next to my name.

"Hello Miss Laurie!"

Without looking up, I know Ticket-Ticket is standing there, twinkling above my head.  He came back.  I force out a smile:

"Hello Tic… "

Good God!  I stop myself just in time: I almost called the man "Ticket-Ticket" to his face!  He frowns but carries on just the same:

"I saw you hopping onboard, a little while ago.  You look gloomy."

"Yes.  It's just one of those days..."

"Ah, yes.  We all have those.  Don't worry.  I'm sure everything will turn out fine."

"Sure thing."

Ticket-Ticket winks at me benevolently before turning on his heels and moving away again, stumbling off in little jolts and jumps with every budge and shift of the wagon.  An infinite wave of gratitude proceeds from me to him.  He did me a lot of good with his kind intervention.

8

We're supposed to leave for the beer bash in half an hour and meet up with the others there. I'm going with Nicky, of course, but as far as I could tell over the phone, she's still pissed off about seeing Maude again. In multiples.

Nicky arrives at my house at about 7:30. When I get in her car, I realize right away that from pissed, she's now progressed to fuming. She's had time to think on the way over:

"Shit. Maude's gonna be all over me the second we get in. I just know it."

I understand Nicky's plight better than she thinks. I've got my own misgivings: I've only just now realized that I don't even know for sure if Larry will be there or not. I never thought to actually ask and find out. Meanwhile, Nicky's still juggling a mixture of jitters and despair:

"I know the whole thing's gonna be a nightmare."

"Look it's not like you owe Maude anything, Nicky. So stop worrying about her."

Nicky looks at me, peeved:

"That's funny. You really think she'll stay put? She'll be right there, right on my heels all the livelong night. Shit. I should've stayed home."

"Maybe she won't even be there…"

"She *told* me she'd be there!"

"I know, I know, but it's Maude. You know how she is."

"And you... You just want to go there to screw Larry..."

I'd like to deny this, if only feebly, but Nicky's on a roll:

"One thing's for sure: if Maude knows I'm coming, she'll be there no matter what."

Poor Nicky. I wish I could say something to comfort her and feed her hopes that Maude won't attend, but it's useless: I want Maude to be there. Yes, I hope she'll be there with all my heart because I know that Larry, if he comes at all, will be coming with Maude. They're always going to parties together, the pair of them. I know it's selfish, but I can't wait to get there, to be there. Poor Nicky. Because now she's going against her will, she drives verrrrrry slowly, taking all the time in the world just to round a corner. She lights a cigarette, extending a lazy hand towards the dashboard to change radio stations. We stop at a light on Henri-Bourassa. Nicky's not the type to open herself up bluntly, like me; she's more reserved, guarded, always retiring within herself. Now however, I can plainly see the delayed effects of Maude-anticipation on her face: Nicky's very real anguish bares itself momentarily, obvious in her eyes, in the way she swallows through her constricted throat. A pang of guilt runs through me.

"Okay Nicky. If you want to go back home, just turn back. It's okay."

My voice is calm, composed, because I'm absolutely sincere. I'd like to see Larry again, but not like that. It's not worth it if it means Nicky has to die a slow death just getting there. No, he's not worth it. We stop at a light. Nicky exhales her cigarette smoke and purses her lips. She thinks for a few seconds, then her eyes light up. Her usual rebellious spirit springs up again, out of nowhere.

"No, that's it. I've made up my mind: we're going! Sorry Laurie… I know I'm seesawing all over the place, but I'm just under a lot of stress, you know."

"I know! The *whole* thing's stressful if you ask me."

Putting inner jubilation aside, I add:

"But I stand by what I said: if you want us to leave, we leave. Just say when, and we'll go, even if we've only been there two minutes."

Nicky glances at me, gratefully but only furtively, because the traffic lights change and we're moving again. Traffic's denser too. Nicky's lips curl on a smile, her features more relaxed.

"All right. We leave whenever we want!"

She said that with a contagious sigh of relief. I feel much calmer myself. It's going to be a nice evening.

Nicky's old college towers in the night like a formidable pallid cathedral. We can see it clearly now, looming in the distance; white spotlights are trained on its façade, giving it the cadaverous air of a haunted house. Its tall spires pierce the sky like silver spikes, all white and scary, but otherwise the rest of the college, including its long rows of sallow-lighted windows, is swallowed by the dark of night; only the first floor is animated. Here, larger windows violently let out crowd noises, loud muffled music and swaying colored lights. That's where the beer bash's at. I feel like throwing up.

We park, get out of the car and eventually fall in the line-up outside. Pure waiting agony. High stress often induces silence, and Nicky and I remain accordingly quiet. I'm absorbed internally. For the past few seconds, I've been thinking one step removed from Larry; I've been thinking about someone else. For one moment, just one, I think about another guy. In my past, there's Paul. We kind of lost track of each other after high school. There's something between us that never really got started, something that's not quite finished yet. I wonder, only for a moment, if he'll be here tonight – but then Larry takes center stage in my thoughts again and that's that.

I look at Nicky. Just by the expression she has on, I can tell she's already maxing out; eyes glum, teeth clenched, she's been monosyllabically commenting every five minutes, not a good sign, with two or three furtive elbow jabs when she thought she saw someone she thought we might know. I haven't seen anybody worth mentioning yet, to be honest. Some faces look familiar, but not really. Everybody's smiling left, right and center; with our fixed features, Nicky and I clash like two Bambis on a highway. I'm thinking about how cold it's starting to get when somebody suddenly taps me on the shoulder; my heart jumps in my throat with the full force of utter surprise.

"Hey Laurie! What's up?"

Turning to face my interlocutor, I already know who it is: Loni Bouchard. Nicky and I met Loni in high school. With her long frizzed-out hair, bulging bubbly eyes and large evil smile, Loni moves in on us with her legendary lack of diplomacy.

"Loni, hey… How are you?"

My voice sounds like it's coming from a great distance. Loni smiles at us sideways:

"Laurie and Nicky… Still and always together? As usual."

I frown, half-insulted:

""As usual"? What's that supposed to mean?"

I instantly wish I could take that back. In the five or six years I've known her, Loni's never once acted normally; she's always either planning or playing a nasty trick on unsuspecting victims, always on to something, and rarely something legal. I've seen her scream "Fuck the hell off, fatso!" right in the face of a three-hundred pound bouncer who was throwing her out of a bar after she fist-fought a coke dealer who was also one of her exes. I've seen her generously spread one of her more gooey bogies across an entire bus window and snort loud enough to empty the seats of all passengers in our immediate vicinity.

Now she's looking at me, chewing a massive wad of gum and rolling some hash between her yellow fingers. Her eyes are aggressive, her voice, hard:

"Laurie and Nicky, Nicky and Laurie. Same thing. I mean you're always together."

"Oh, I see."

Because I've softened my tone, Loni switches modes and proudly brandishes her hash, still stuck between her thumb and index. She shows it off to Nicky, who answers with a weak smile:

"You see that? Guess where I got it?"

Quickly losing interest, I look over Loni's shoulder, past her and beyond other people, checking for anyone or anything resembling Larry, or even Maude. Politely, Nicky asks:

"Where did you get it?"

"I stole it from Bernie while he was talking to Cedric."

Paf!  I instantly double back to the conversation. As expected, Nicky looks aghast.  All-engrossed by the hash she's now examining suspiciously, Loni is oblivious to the drama unfolding.  I wait for Nicky to speak or make a move, but she's slipped into full-metabolic coma.  I take the lead:

"Cedric?  Really?  He's here then?"

Loni barely looks up.

"Yeah, he's here.  He's already inside with his friends.  I saw them before they went in."

"Why didn't you go in with them?"

"I don't have a ticket.  But I have a plan.  You guys have tickets?"

I nod.  Nicky's still immobile, transfixed – then, suddenly, she speaks:

"Okay, that's it.  We're leaving."

Oh no.  Nicky has spoken.  Has spoken and is on the move: fiercely throwing her hair back, she spins around and ejects out of the line-up, on a sprint.

"Nicky!!!"

I run after her, trying to catch up.  While Loni follows us, surprised, Nicky turns to me quickly, talking in a feverish hush before Loni can hear her:

"Listen, Laurie.  I know you want to see Larry, but Maude AND Cedric?  No way.  I just can't handle that. There's no way."

Loni pulls up.

"Hey, what's your problem?  You're leaving?"

I look at Nicky again.  She's eyeing the college with absolute dread.  Loni croaks:

"If you're leaving, I'll take your tickets."

Neither Nicky nor I answer – because at that same, exact and very moment, one of the beer bash organizers sticks his head out of the main doors. He yells, loud enough to be heard by everyone in the line-up:

"Full house, folks! Sorry. If you have tickets, ask for a refund on Monday."

That's it. He closes the door while around us many cries of protest burst forth. Nicky turns to me, face undone.

"You see. We can't go in anyway… Let's just go home."

Loni, tight-lipped until now, starts laughing sarcastically.

"Wow. You girls really give up fast."

I complain:

"The guy *just said* they're not letting anyone else in."

"Who cares about him? Come on."

Her step determined, Loni walks back to the college, with the two of us behind her in uneasy tow. Soon running stealthily alongside the building, she surveys the wall facing us as Nicky and I follow her, exchanging puzzled looks. We skip over some loose refuse, dispersed piles of garbage, and bypass three big trashcans which Loni sends reeling with some fracas after one swift kick of the boot. The smell's awful. A streetlamp dying nearby douses us with its blueish, evaporating light. Loni slows down:

"I thought it was here somewhere…"

Facing us now is a sort of garden-shed extension, jutting out of the main hall. Loni hits it a couple of times, in various places.  Nothing.  She hits it again.  This time, the sound was different, hollow.  Loni stops and smiles at us:

"Are you ready to party, girls?"

She knocks on the shed again, three times.  Against all expectations, a door suddenly opens, spewing a torrent of decibels and one lone fuzzy-bearded guy.  He looks younger than us; peering into his molten composure however, one can tell he's been partying longer.  Instead of sounding the alarm, he mumbles:

"Don't have tickets?  No problem.  Get in."

## 9

A beer bash, as the name implies, is a big booze binge. People usually try to get there early to get topped up many times over before unwinding in a mosh pit or the odd rigadoon, when the DJ feels folkloric. The party itself always takes place in the cafeteria: tables are pushed up against the wall to give leeway to an improvised dance-floor, where, initially at least, people prefer to stand and talk or talk and drink.

We slyly move onto the premises. There's already an interminable line of people waiting for beer coupons; in an effort to slow down alcohol consumption, organizers force students to buy coupons and line-up again to exchange them for beer, at another counter. Ha! That was before Loni out-organized the entire system: once inside, she heads straight for the coupon line, shoving people aside, bullying and coaxing others, rapidly building a whole network of coupon-scalping operatives. In the course of the next few hours, she'll slowly raise her prices, preying on students too lazy to wait in line or too drunk to realize they're getting ripped off. Even at a conservative estimate, Loni's take for the night will account for at least one quarter of tomorrow's hangovers.

I smile widely as I peer into the crowd; bevies of partygoers move, shift and swarm together in full collective symbiosis while ear-splittingly loud music and rainbows of lights sweep the air. I'm so much in my element, it's almost orgasmic. Nicky pulls on my sleeve:

"Should we buy our coupons now?"

One look at the queue: Loni is busy cutting in front of four students she's been remorselessly intimidating with her predatory allure.  I shake my head:

"Nah, look at that line-up.  It's two miles long.  Let's wait."

"Yeah but I'll need some beer for courage, you know, before I can face Maude.  Or Cedric."

After some deliberation, I give in:

"Okay.  But stay close so we don't lose each other."

I start towards the coupon line with Nicky following in convoy, both of us elbowing our way through.  We walk past a poster that says "Drug-taking forbidden here".  Someone crossed out "forbidden".  A great evening lies in wait, I'm sure!  What's more, I swear I've never seen so many good-looking guys all at the same place at the same time.  Unparalleled.  Beer bashes are known for that, but still, this year's a good vintage...  I've already noticed three or four engaging males in the last three or four seconds.  Nicky's also spotted them; out of the corner of my eye, I can see her twirling her hair back with that little sexy air she can put on.  I prefer to make my play on the quiet.  Manoeuvring through the crowd, I exploit every opportunity to augment proximity, brushing up against potential conquests, saying "Sorry..." as I move past, pretending I have to bodily handle them because of some imaginary crowd movement.  It works, too.  I immediately collect two or three flattered smiles.

Really, the evening's off to a tremendous start, I must say, and that's with or without Larry, or with or without anybody that fits his description, even remotely.  Anyway he must've changed since last I saw him.  I'm not even sure I'll recognize him: as I recall, he had very short hair, was clean-shaven, and his pants were torn because he'd unstitched the seams to make them longer. I thought it gave him a nice look. Of course, I'm biased. I just think he's got something, a je ne sais quoi. Nicky begs to differ; she says Larry looks like a mosquito. She never likes any guys I like. How she manages to do this, I'm sure I don't know, because I like variety: short, tall, thin, plump, brunette, blond, bald, red-headed, tanned, facial hair, no hair, very hairy, name it. When it comes to men, I'm open-minded, but that's about all I am: my experience in the matter is still pretty limited. I mean I can still count my suitors on the fingers of one hand. Nicky, on the other hand, is hyperbolically picky. She'd be able to write a three-page list (single-spaced) on her preselection requirements. And I'm not saying that just for effect; she actually did that once.

Before we can get in line, Loni intercepts us, a bunch of coupons under each arm and a satisfied grin on her face:

"There you go, girls!"

She sells us three coupons each, at a discount. A generous gesture on her part, considering how rapacious she's been, getting her loot by hook and crook. We watch her disappear into the crowd, and then head together for the beer counter and the all-important coupon/beer exchange. I'm glad to see Nicky's completely regained her footing. I myself feel on top form. I place my order, making eye-contact with the guy behind the counter, a tall lanky type with long hair, when Nicky elbows me right in the stomach:

"Laurie, they're here."

Her face now contorted by very real anxiety, Nicky looks off to a faraway point. I tail her gaze and catch sight of a table, tucked at the far end of the room. There, sitting together, are Cynthia, Sharon, Guss… and Maude.

Nicky turns to me with an expression that says a lot about her intentions of drinking herself into acute despondency. Feeling a twinge of sorrow, I take a beer from the lanky guy: all I know is that Larry's not here. I pick myself up and lead the way towards our friends. Nicky tags along half-heartedly. As we plod through to get over there, all I see is that Larry's not there, Larry's not there, Larry's not there. As we get closer, I can see other people hanging around in the background (I'm comfortably short-sighted): Gamache, Yohan, Miguel… No, no Larry. They're all here. Except him.

Of course, Maude sees us first, to Nicky's eternal delight.

"Hey, Nicky, Laurie! Hey, we're over here!"

The whole group turns toward us; we're greeted warmly. Maude goes out of her way to meet up with Nicky, who avoids contact by making a hard left and embracing Sharon instead. Maude falls back on me, planting two wet kisses on my cheeks:

"How are you Maude? You haven't changed a bit."

She laughs and answers without listening, absorbed by Nicky's propinquity:

"How are you, Laurie?"

"I'm good. And you?"

"So how are you, Laurie?"

"Err, I'm good, Maude, thanks."

God. Poor Maude, she's got it really bad. Leaving her behind, still gushing over Nicky, I nod a little stiffly to Miguel and Gamache, both of whom are conscientiously rolling joints under the table. I elect to sit between Cyn and Yohan. Meanwhile, Nicky struggles to say hi to Maude, who receives this cold salutation with transports of jubilation. I've been here chatting for, what, about two thirds of a minute, when I suddenly feel uneasy, like I'm being watched. Closely. It's coming from the left. Squinting in the darkness, I realize that my discomfort comes from Guss, seated in the remotest corner. He's been staring at me since I got here. I smile at him, waving my hand. He gets up to come over while I finish exchanging the usual niceties with Cyn and Yohan.

I met Guss the same year as Larry. His real name is Fred Guillet-Gosselin; the nickname comes from the contraction of the first syllables of his double-barrel name. Easy to remember. It's Yohan who christened Guss "Guss". This was to differentiate him from Gamache, who's another Fred, even though no one ever calls either one of them Fred. Back in high school, Guss was a semi-celebrity, a kind of mythical figure because:

a) He had a cool nickname
b) He had a car
and c) He threw parties at his parents' house every weekend (condolences to neighbors).

His parents put up with anything, be it alcohol, dope or the impromptu excavation of their pantry. The first time I met Guss was at one of those parties, at his house. He sat next to me, we started talking; the connection between us was instantaneous, natural. I liked him right away. He was funny, intelligent, different but on the same wavelength as me. As time went by, we saw each other often, often alone. He made me laugh a lot and brought me along when he went garage-sale hunting on Saturday mornings (he got up early for that express purpose). In our high school parking lot, the arrival of his red car invariably caused a commotion. Guss had around him a large herd of perpetual parasites because he had in his possession a constant flow of cheap weed and was incapable of turning anyone down. He never said no to anybody, least of all me; he was in love. I knew that but I played innocent, flirting outrageously with him before leaving him with himself. I know, that's mean, but I forgive myself because I was young(er). I didn't know any better. Anyway, I was already starting to take an interest in Larry, even back then, so. Poor Guss. He suffered in silence, rendered defenseless by his terrible desire to be loved and my endless sexless overtures. Although I felt guilty about how I treated him, I did nothing to repent or amend, and our friendship understandably crumbled along the way.

Seeing him again tonight moves me. Guss looks at people as he always has, with the same fixed interest, the same ambivalent awkwardness. He says hi to Nicky as he passes her, kissing her cheeks. Nicky shoots me a glance over his shoulder. Instead of waiting, I take the initiative of getting up to greet him, to ease his discomfort.

"Hey Guss, how are you?"

My tone is tender, and I also cheek-kiss him gently. Beaming, he answers.

"Laurie, hi. I'm doing okay. You?"

"Okay. You look good."

"Yeah? Thanks. You too. It's been a long time…"

"Yeah. So what are you up to, Guss?"

"Oh, nothing much…"

"Ah…"

"I'm working in an apartment complex in St. Michel. I've got an apartment there now."

I'm surprised.

"You moved?"

He laughs.

"Yes. You're still living with your mommy?"

His voice is gratuitously disdainful. Especially on the words "still" and "mommy". I make it a point to ignore this.

"Yes, well, I'm still in school."

"Getting your degree."

"Yes, I'm almost done. I'll be graduating in a few months."

As I say this, I swath him on the shoulder, to share with him my happy thought of leaving school behind forever. As it extends from me however, my little gesture morphs into a desire for closeness. The thing passes between Guss and I like a mutual interrogation. It's been such a long time since I've seen him. I realize now that I've actually, genuinely missed him.

"I've missed you, Guss…"

I'm so deeply sincere, I can even feel my eyes watering. The whole thing could be a high moment of real emotion, if it weren't for what happens next: in a completely unexpected move, Guss pulls away from me and shuts himself off. I look on, surprised, as he barricades himself within himself, his face grave, his eyes elsewhere, overcast.  Taking a very nonchalant swig of his beer, he follows that up with:

"Really?  That's not like you…"

I understand now: he's still angry.  He resents the fact that I've had other interests, that I had affection for him and not desire.  I understand that, but tonight, I don't feel like feeling guilty all over again.  I don't want to think about other people's misguided hopes – I've still got mine to worry about.

I suddenly wish I could get away from Guss as fast as possible.  I'd like to drop him right there, on the spot, ignoring his bitterness and martyr-like scowl.  Before I can move on that, behind him the crowd parts.  In comes a guy who's looking straight at me while approaching us.  I can't see who it is: my myopia again.

Guss lifts his cigarette pack in front of my eyes, blocking the view:

"Want a smoke?"

I shake my head bluntly, annoyed, and Guss exhales from the cigarette he just lit.  When the curls of smoke dissipate, the guy who was walking towards us approaches again.  I frown, but he smiles.  Oh God, now I see him.  It's Larry.  Taller, more muscular, less pubescent, with longer hair and a goatee.  It's Larry.  The manly version.

A searing flash of ecstasy shoots right through me but I immediately cork any outward manifestation.  Years of experience feigning indifference enable me to save face graciously.  I can even echo Larry's laid-back smile, which he presses against my cheek as he kisses and embraces me:

"Laurie…  Wow!  How are you?"

He hugs me very tightly. Oh God, dear God, oh God. I can see Guss glaring at us with his own personal brand of silent sarcasm, but I don't care. Larry lets go of me and I answer placidly:

"I'm doing okay. You?"

"Doing okay also. I saw you back at the beer counter, you and Nicky. You just got here?"

"Yes, a couple of minutes ago."

"You look cute with your little pigtails."

I use all my powers of resistance to prevent the catastrophe of blushing on the outside. Thank God-Almighty I decided to wear my hair up in pigtails. With his usual people-pleaser countermove, Guss offers Larry a cigarette, which Larry accepts without hesitation. I can see him clearly now, Larry. Up close, he looks old, older I mean, in a nice way. Facial hair gives him a virile veneer I've never associated with him before. He's wearing a kind of padded flannel shirt that looks ridiculous, but I completely smooth over this detail when he looks at me again through the smoke he expels:

"So? What's new?"

What's new? What's new… Shit! Oh no. Oh my God. Nothing's new! What's new? School? No. Work? No, that's not new. HA! What else?!? School?!!? Work?!!? No, there's nothing new! Nothing!!! Shit, I've got nothing to say!!!

I pretend I'm intrigued by something off in the distance, answering (apparently) absent-mindedly:

"Oh, not much… You?"

Larry smiles again. Phew.

"Me? Nothing much either. I've gone back to school. I've decided to try and finish high school after all."

"Really?"

"Yeah. Actually, it was you, Laurie, that gave me the incentive."

I gave him the incentive? The incentive for what? Oh yes, school! Laurie, stay focused, stay focused, listen to what the man's saying, good grief, think straight!

"I never knew that, Larry. How come?"

Keep cool, keep cool.

"When you were accepted in Literature, you were so passionate about your classes, you made it sound so important, it got me thinking…"

I'd love to get him thinking all right… God, focus girl! I laugh, detached:

"Oh, I think your timing's off, Larry! I'm actually thinking of quitting it all. I hate school!"

He laughs. God, even his voice is deeper. God in heaven.

"Come on, don't say that to me now! You'll ruin any good intentions I have."

While he's talking, he grazes my abdomen with his hand. My heart skips all kinds of beats. I look at him, destabilized: of course, he looks away, hiding his expression by looking at people on the dance-floor. I take the opportunity to recompose my features. Only Guss, his face taunt and tight, witnessed my obvious emotional turmoil. Nicky passes between him and Larry, ready to fetch herself a second beer. Larry leans towards her:

"Hi there, Veronica!"

Nicky stops dead in her tracks, surprised.

"Larry?  My God, long time no see, man."

She immediately zooms in on his flannel shirt:

"What the hell's that?  You look like a freakin' lumberjack!"

While Larry crumples, Nicky laughs inconsiderately before heading straight for the beer counter.  Retreating to a corner, Larry gets rid of the offensive flannel garment at once, throwing it on our pile of coats; he looks better in a T-shirt anyway.  Guss laughs meanly and takes Nicky's empty seat at the table.  Wary of being left alone with Larry, and having nothing to say to him, as I've discovered, I follow Guss instead and sit next to him; this also gives me the chance to chat with Sharon.  Larry sits down between Miguel and Yohan, opposite me.  It's funny, but all of a sudden, I'd like for Larry to not be here, I'd like for him to leave, to go, go away, right now, so I can have a nice, relaxed, pleasant evening.

# 10

How predictable.  It happens when Nicky comes back from the beer counter.  She's walking with her usual self-confidence, throwing her hair back carelessly.  When she sees her coming, Maude springs out of her seat in full greeting stance again, but as she gets up, there's a collision: Maude runs right into Cedric who was coming over to say hello, not noticing Nicky who was coming up behind him.  It all happens very quickly: Cedric's "Hey Maude!" overlaps with Maude's gleeful "Nicky!" and there it is: Nicky and Cedric come face-to-face.

Nicky stops dead in her tracks, startled, but also because Maude stands in the way.  Cedric, visibly flustered, turns back on his heels and sprints off in a way that leaves no doubt as to his extreme embarrassment.  While he evaporates in the crowd, Nicky glares at Maude, her face now psychopathic, motioning her out of the way with a curt "Sorry".  That "Sorry" is so piercingly-loud, we all clearly hear it, even over the blaring music.  The word acts on Maude like a ton of bricks; she's hit with it full-frontal, like a stab in the heart.

Nicky walks on, rolling her eyes at me to communicate absolute exasperation.  I smile, showing I've seen and grasped the meaning of events playing out.  Somehow however, I know my smile's forced.  I feel for Maude.  Not that she deserves it necessarily.  She's a strange one, Maude: except for her endearing, feverish love pleas, she's not really a nice person.  Among her many faults, she steals, from everybody.  Maude's a real, clinical kleptomaniac, she can't help it.  She steals what she eats, wears or sells back, she hijacks and usurps what she has, had, or gives away, she pockets money from Yohan, Gamache, Miguel and Larry when they're too stoned to know any better, she pillages us girls by borrowing money she never repays, she takes cigarettes from our packs and swears otherwise afterwards, even when someone actually catches her in the act. She also stole from Nicky, the night they had their infamous threesome. She took money from her purse while Nicky was putting her clothes back on. It's a medical condition or something.

I look at Maude now as she sits with Gamache, laughing as if nothing happened, making jokes, pretending she's not hurt by Nicky's very public brush-off. Nervously, she keeps on pulling a strand of hair behind one of her ears; that's what betrays her. All of her heartache is there, in that little unconscious gesture.

"She should know better by now: Nicky's not interested."

That's Guss, sitting next to me; he too saw what happened. He bites his lower lip and shakes his head sadly, looking at Maude. We're all aware of the little human drama unfolding before us. Still sitting with Cyn and Sharon, Nicky has now begun to sigh wearily between halts in conversations. I know, just by looking at her, that our time here is drawing to an end. I know that, very soon, she'll tell me "We're leaving!", and I'll have to leave.

I look over at Larry. He's in a deep tête-à-tête with Miguel; they're talking in undertones, all in subdued affection, laughing together and often patting each other's backs. When a thin guy with short hair comes up to them however, they change gears right away: loud now, with big handshakes, they offer joyous how-are-yous to the newcomer. I wonder for a moment if that could be Paul, my guy-friend from high school, the one I was thinking about earlier on – but no, it's someone else.

The person in question looks familiar but I can't place him. From the outset, he seems kind and smart, with affable features and a shrewd little twinkle in his eyes. He's wearing a ring on his ring finger. This detail catches my attention while he's talking animatedly, holding two glasses of beer with one hand, looking through his pockets for a pack of matches with the other – this is to service Larry, who just asked him for a light.

It's strange. This guy totally clashes with the people around us: in our sea of cool-looking waste-heads, his tidy profile stands as a complete incoherence. Still, there's something intriguing there, a sort of proud and independent self-affirmation. He laughs a lot and his voice too sounds familiar. He's still chatting with Larry and Miguel when a girl with ironed-flat hippie hair slips between them, kissing every guy hello, alternately. A shot of pure unmitigated jealousy hits me right in the stomach. The new guy looks at the girl warmly, handing her one of the beers he's holding. I elbow Guss:

"Hey, who's the guy talking with Miguel?"

I know this is an obvious circumnavigation around what I really mean ("Who's the guy with Larry"), but I want to spare whatever's left of Guss' feelings, as well as my own dignity. Susceptible as always, Guss squints into the crowd:

"Him? That's Peter Whosit – Boyard, Godard, Follard, or something…"

"Peter?"

I frown.  I'm sure I know that guy.  Guss offers some precision:

"Yeah, you know, Peter."

"Okay…"

"You know, everyone calls him "Peetee".  He used to tag along with us back in the days, you know, with Yohan and Gamache."

I look at this Peter again.  This time, I recognize him:

"Ah, yeah!  Peter: that's the guy who threw Yohan's beer in his face that night?"

"That's it."

Hmm.  Yes, I remember now.  Peter.

Yohan, who heard his name spoken between us, joins our discussion:

"What's that?  You're talking about me?"

I smile:

"Do you remember when Peter, the guy over there, threw your beer in your face?"

Yohan roars with laughter.  It's contagious.  Guss and I start laughing too.  Yohan shakes his head like he's incredulous:

"Peetee!  He's a crazy son of a bitch!"

And he summons:

"Hey, Peetee!  Peetee!  Come here, you crazy motherfucker!"

Peter looks up, sees us and smiles widely as he recognizes Yohan, gesturing wildly in his direction.  He comes over, bringing with him Larry and Miguel.  The hippie girl got lost somewhere in the interval. Good. Peter smiles:

"Yohan, man!  What news from the front?"

Big tall handshakes.  I shrink a little on my chair when Peter looks at me.  He quickly moves on, fortunately, because Guss has gotten up to shake hands with him even more formally.

"Guss?  Good Lord.  How long has it been?"

"It's been a while."

Peter transfers his attention back to me.  Larry makes the introductions:

"Laurie, that's Peter.  Peetee, that's Laurie, you remember?  She used to party with us."

With a charming smile, Peter extends his beringed hand:

"No, I don't recall…"

Great.

"…how do you do?"

"Hi, Peter."

That's it.  Peter, Yohan, Larry and Miguel resume their reminiscences while I finish my beer and the hippie girl comes traipsing back again, draping her arms around Peter's neck.

"I guess she's the girlfriend."

I wanted to think that privately but said it out loud. I regret this right away because Guss is still within earshot. As expected, his legendary touchiness flies in overdrive:

"The girl?  I don't know.  His girlfriend?  Why? What's that to you?"

I knew it.  I just hate that.  I hate that little sarcastic tone infecting all those little sentences.  I've had enough:

"What's your problem?"

Guss looks genuinely surprised:

"What do you mean?"

"You're always mean to me.   What's your problem?"

He grins awkwardly.  Miguel pulls away from his conversation with the other guys.  He turns to us:

"Fighting again you two?"

"It's not me, it's him!  He gets on my nerves with his little snide attacks…"

Guss gets up:

"You really piss me off, Laurie!"

He says that through a fake laugh, trying to preserve his grandeur, but when our eyes meet again, I know, from years of experience of looking into them, that he really means what he said.  He turns away, guzzling his beer.  Then he looks at me one last time:

"I'm going to the bathroom."

"Fall in."

My voice is dry, full of contempt.  Guss shrugs and dwindles away in the crowd.  Miguel takes his seat and lights a cigarette.  I ponder the incident, twirling my empty beer glass in my hands.

"You want one?"

Miguel offers me a cigarette from his pack.

"No thanks.  I've stopped smoking."

I get up.  I need another beer.

## 11

Back at the beer counter, a girl in a tight top serves me. The tall thin guy I was flirting with before is nowhere to be found. Just as I thought: the whole evening is going down the drain, slowly but surely: Larry ignores me, the hippie girl very successfully glues herself to every guy in town, and Guss has, I'm sure, great reserves of untapped sarcastic remarks to yet unspool. God. It's only 9:42 and I'm already climaxing on extreme boredom. And, oh yes, let's not forget my presentation, on Tuesday. Yeah. I should've stayed home. I should've known Larry's interest in me could only be limited to…

"Your third beer?"

Err. That's Larry, pit-stopping as well. I look down at my full glass.

"No, second one."

"Only two ales? Oh come on, Laurie. You need a helping hand…"

With that, he takes the beer off me and gulps down a sumptuous quarter of a glass, winking at me playfully over the rim. All my mournful thoughts dissipate. Larry hands me back my glass, licking the foam over his lips. Dear God. Instead of waiting for him while he gets his own beverage from the counter, I slip away and escape out of his reach, throwing myself on the dance-floor where I join up with Sharon, Nicky, Maude and Guss. They all smile when they see me, even Guss.

I had no choice, for Larry. I mean, I had to get away: his lip-licking thing was way too risqué. I don't like to burn with desire in front of anybody, especially not him.

No.  I'm better off here dancing, lost in the melee; even with a three-quarters-full glass of beer, I'm better off here, melting in music.

While we all gyrate around, I see Cedric moving past, behind Nicky.  He gives her a sideway glance to which Nicky reacts, her face momentarily creased with worry.  When he's gone, she dispatches a hand in my direction and pulls me in as I lend an ear to her plea:

"Laurie!  Did you see Cedric?  He just walked by."

"Yes, I saw him.  What is it?"

"Laurie!  I have to go!"

There it is: the signal.  The moment when Nicky decides we have to leave.  I stop dancing:

"Are you sure?  I mean, I just bought a beer here…"

Nicky looks at me strangely, smiling too much. There's something unusual in her gaze.

"No, Laurie, you don't understand: I have to go talk to Cedric!"

I instinctively recoil:

"What?!?  What do you mean "talk"?"

"I have to do it!  I just have to talk to him!"

She looks at me with all the determination in the world, plus the five beers she's had so far.  Although I can see disaster spelled all over this idea, I say nothing.  I'm lost for words anyway.  I know, just by looking at her, that Nicky will not back down.  Not in this state, not now that her decision's made.  I look over at Maude, still dancing unsuspectingly.  Nicky takes me in her arms:

"Wish me luck…"

She lets go of me and leaves.  I try to recompose my features into a relaxed mask, to cover for her, to pretend nothing's going on, protecting her from all inquiries, specifically Maude's. My little plan works; nobody raises an eyebrow at Nicky's abrupt exit, nobody guesses at my unease.

I've only just started dancing again when there's a sudden pelvic motion leading my own. And a hand on my waist. Looking down, I recognize Larry's sleeve: he's holding me, tightly pressed against him, dancing behind me, rhythmically moving my body with his. The dance-floor's jam-packed now; there's so many people around, no one can see us. Not Maude, not Guss, not anyone. No one can see me smiling, no one sees me turning to face Larry who smiles back, flirt exposed:

"I wanna dance with you…"

I slip into tease-mode too, just to keep a handle on things:

"You like dancing with me Larry?"

"Yeah, you're a good dancer…"

I honestly don't know where all this is coming from, the big obvious exchange of seductive platitudes. It's like we suddenly accessed the same roadmap to superficial floor-sex, Larry and I. We're a little drunk, that's all it is really, but still I try to uncensor myself as much as possible. I move languidly, or try to anyway, and Larry returns the favor:

"It's been a while since we danced together."

"We've never danced together, Larry."

"No, we did. New Year's Eve, two years ago, at my house…"

"Oh, that's right. I forgot."

Of course, I'm lying shamelessly. I remember everything; every single detail of that night – but before I can travel further down that memory lane, I notice how something seems out of place. I can't tell what's going on yet, I can't concentrate. To make matters worse, Larry folds me in his arms completely, burying his face in my neck. His warm breath, half-open mouth, and hands sliding down my backside…

"God, it's been so long…"

He said that with a long sigh. I try closing my eyes, getting lost in the moment – but I can't. Something's wrong now, I know it. It comes from outside, from around us, like someone's been hit head-on; something just punched the air. It's a weird impression, shared by Sharon, Guss and even Larry himself. We all felt it because we're now all looking at each other with the same perplexed air. Then I see her: Maude. Her features flattened, thrown back in unspeakable rage, eyes bulging, she stares at a fixed point. Through a fissure in the crowd, she just spotted Nicky and Cedric, caught in the obvious splendor of a serious conversation. It's apparent to me, as well as to the others, and more so perhaps to Maude, that Nicky and Cedric are talking about something that concerns *them*. Exclusively.

Like an enraged, wounded animal, Maude lunges for attack. In a split-second impulse, we all tackle her, Sharon, Guss, Larry and me, we drop everything and grab Maude by the arm, by her hair, by her shirt, anything.

"Maude! Maude!! Stop!!!"

"I'll kill those two fuckers! I'll kill 'em!"

People move away from us; we're there, struggling to rein in Maude like a furious nucleus in the middle of a naked clearing on the dance-floor. Gamache and Miguel sprint over and help us bring Maude back to our table. The

DJ switches tunes, the party resumes, the crowd closes behind us, but Maude's still out of control.  Frothing at the mouth, she screams:

"Let go of me, get off me you fuckers!!!"

She's crying, but it's out of blind rage.  Gamache, Miguel and Larry finally manage to overcome her.  I leave them and head straight for Nicky, to give her some warning.  Her big conversation with Cedric is over anyway; she's alone now.

"Veronica!  Maude's gone insane!"

Nicky stares at me, wide-eyed.

"What?"

"She saw you talking to Cedric and she lost her mind.  We had to pin her down, all of us!"

"I can speak to whoever I want, whenever I want."

I look at Nicky, at her little mutinous air, staring at me with that calm self-assurance of hers.  Looking back at our table, through the meandering crowd, I see Maude again: she's settled down, her head plunged deep into her hands.  Larry's talking to her, leaning in kindly, but the others have all gone back to their chats and beers, like nothing happened.  It's all over.

## 12

After that, needless to say, the rest of the evening fell through. Nicky shut herself off, her silence magnified by Maude's many desperate glances; I assisted Sharon while she vomited in a toilet; an angry Guss stormed out after Gamache sold him weak weed; and Larry and Miguel went outside to drop acid and never found their way back in. That's when Nicky and I decided to call it quits. Loads of fun, yes indeed.

This morning, as soon as I enter the lifeless void of the Community Center, J.F. detects my dejection. He asks anyway:

"So? How was the party?"

He's busy picking up basketballs in the gym. His voice reverberates back to me, echo, while I crouch outside my office. I hate working weekends. There's even less to do than during the week, if that's at all possible. There's absolutely nobody around. The only disruption in this dead environment comes from the "vrrrrrrrrrrrr" of the generator. Eight hours of that can make anybody bust a spring.

J.F. waits. In my mind, the answer to his question has trouble getting words to match. I think back to the bash; I see Larry in high resolution again, in full close-up, an indefinite gaze floating above his vaporous smile. His spaced-out approach is so malleable, it can be made to mean anything. I hate not knowing what he thinks. Even when he's being nice, Larry always sprinkles his voice with an unctuous hint of ambiguity. Hence my verdict:

"The party sucked."

"What about the gorgeous Mr. Larry?"

"He was there. And I told you already, he's not gorgeous."

"He was there? So? What happened?"

I hesitate but the answer comes out ahead of me:

"Nothing."

J.F. rears up, a basketball under each arm and a puzzled look on his face.

"What do you mean, "nothing"?"

I shrug disdainfully. I loathe to admit it, but the total sum of Larry's little side-glances, quivering whispers and wandering hands, all those insinuations that passed between us like so many things left unsaid, don't really amount to much, to be honest.

J.F. is sincerely sorry for me:

"Oh… And I thought you spent last night in a sex festival…"

Inertia compels J.F. to spend a lot of time trying to reach unfathomable depths of mental depravity. I usually manage to keep up with him, but today, even though I laugh after his remark, it's just to give myself some countenance:

"A sex festival? A boredom festival, more like. What a complete yawn. I should've stayed home doing homework. That would've been more interesting."

J.F. smiles and puts away the basketballs in garage number four. There are exactly twenty-four garages at the Community Center, seventeen storage lockers, eight locker rooms, six offices, one elevator, two hundred and forty locks with matching keys, one reception hall, two gymnasiums, one weight-lifting room, plus my fishbowl of an office. Inertia once compelled me to reach supreme heights of mental activity and count it all out.  J.F. walks over to me:

"I don't get it.  You were so psyched about seeing him again."

"You'd think."

"Oh, come on!  Don't fake me out again.  Just last week, you had trouble putting up the badminton nets because you were thinking about him so much.  You can't get enough of that old boyfriend of yours..."

I'd like to reflect, just for a moment here, on how pride and low self-esteem are complexly interwoven, but instead I shoot back:

"Okay.  I thought about him from time to time, that's true, but that's it.  And I've told you a hundred thousand times: he was never my boyfriend, so stop calling him that."

J.F. looks at me like he's getting the info for the first time:

"Weren't you dating at some point?"

"No.  I think I was just an appetizer for him.  Not even a part-time semi-girlfriend.  It's complicated."

"Things look pretty simple to me."

"Of course it's simple from your perspective!  But Larry's… He's complicated.  I never know what he thinks. He's always flashing right and turning left."

"Give me a "For example"."

J.F. closes garage number four, waiting for me to elaborate.  It just so happens that an example is right within reach, still close to memory, preserved in a homemade cocktail of 30% frustration, 70% melancholy:

"Larry's the kind of guy who fondles you for half an hour in a public place but then freezes when we get back to his place, all alone, with everything just right for the thing."

J.F. arches his brow:

"He fondled you in public?"

"Often.  At parties, in bars...  Once in a library, even."

"A library?  Which section?"

J.F. belly-laughs at my expense while I get up, pouting for form.  I go back to my office and J.F. follows me there, looking serenely happy as he sits in the wheelchair we keep for emergencies: slap-shots in a referee's kneecap are more common than people think.  Still feeling down, still sulking, I stay put.  J.F. lazily wheels and rolls to and fro.

"Why don't you just ask him directly?  I mean, ask him why he can't make up his mind…"

"Ask him?  Are you kidding?  That ruins a mood!  Anyway, it's too clear, too precise.  Larry could never face up to that.  The guy's balls hang by a thread…"

The rest of my answer is swallowed up by the phone ringing.  J.F. literally throws himself on the receiver.  Assisting citizens is, for him, pure pleasure:

"Hello, this is the Community Center.  How may I help you?"

J.F.'s plastic professionalism is so perfect, it makes me giggle.  Putting his hand over the mouthpiece, he motions for me to be quiet – but when he says "What do you mean, there's a squirrel in your pool?" with a bewildered expression, I can't help myself: I just roar. J.F. shoos me off.  A squirrel in a pool.  That's exactly what we deal with here at the Community Center.  Local residents often think – and I sympathize here – that calling the City means accessing a wide network of organized and responsible civic workers, employees who are conscientious, hardworking, have relevant diplomas and/or qualifications and experience in their specific field of expertise. Instead of all that, they get me or, if they're lucky, J.F., who's better at customer service: two considerate but immature young people comfortably paid for doing and/or knowing next to nothing.

J.F. refers the guy and his squirrel to the dog pound. When I hear him give out the number, I gesture desperately. He hangs up, then turns to me:

"What?"

"Not the pound! The guy who's in charge is not even in today. It's closed."

"Oh. Well, that's that. Anyway, it's not my job. I'm supposed to be the gym supervisor."

"So why do you keep answering that phone?"

"You're not fast enough."

J.F. looks over at the phone guiltily.

"I'm sure the guy'll call back. Anyway, his pool's empty. It's not like the squirrel's drowning or anything… So? Where were we?"

"I can't get my hands on Larry."

"Right."

J.F. sits back down in his wheelchair to listen to my grievances again.

"I swear, I'm beginning to think something's wrong. How come all my relationships fail? It's like there's a no-fuck zone around me. Like a little automatic mechanism that repels guys I want and attracts those I don't."

"Come on…"

"I'm telling you: I always end up with guys who don't really mean anything to me. And that's on a good day!"

J.F. laughs and propels himself out of the office and into the deserted hall. He does a few wheelies:

"Laurie, I don't want to be nasty or anything, but "Laurie and Larry"? Sounds awful."

"I know. You're right. I just *have* to forget the whole thing."

The phone in the office rings again and I answer: it's the squirrel guy. I transfer him to public security. When I hang up, J.F. rolls back in the office with an extension cord on his knees. I look at him, surprised:

"Where did you get that?"

"What?"

"The extension in your lap. What's it for?"

A little mischievous grin lights J.F.'s symmetrical face. He leaps out of the wheelchair.

"I got it from the janitor's closet. Stay here and watch."

J.F. delicately moves me out of the way and kneels in front of the rickety table I'm supposed to be using as a desk. Winking at me, he plugs the extension in the power outlet in the wall, and then heads for the gym. I tag along, curious. J.F. opens garage number seven. He takes out the old TV set the day-care service uses to entertain and enlighten the children. Struck by a bolt of guilty pleasure, I run off to inspect the hallways while J.F. installs the TV in my office. The hallways are still deserted, the coast is clear, all's well: you could hear a pin drop if it weren't for the "vrrrrrrrrrrrr". When I get back, J.F.'s already lounging in his wheelchair, feet on the table. From the outside, he just looks like he's staring slothfully into space: the TV's half-hidden behind a box of cheerleader pompoms.  When I walk in again, he beams at me radiantly:

"Wait here.  I'll be right back."

J.F. gets up and flattens me against the wall as he rushes out the door.

"Where are you going?"

He disappears into the nearest stairway.  I sit in the office, looking at the church program J.F. was watching. It changes the whole atmosphere, having a TV in here.  It's like having our own little art-deco apartment or something. J.F. comes back, looking profoundly satisfied.  He pulls out two cans of soda and a bottle of vodka from under his shirt.

"Vodka?  J.F.!  Are you insane?"

"Don't sweat."

The City keeps an underground reserve of a few choice alcoholic compounds for anything ranging from carnivals and barbecues to special activities, special days and other special days… There's enough booze here, at the Community Center, for ample sampling sessions, with anyone free to partake without incurring so much as a loose verbal reprimand.  Part-time and full-time employees, blue-collars and white-collars, volunteers and passing benefactors… there's a lot of people drawing at the source.  J.F. just followed suit and took what he felt was owned.

"Cheers!"

As I look on, J.F. wets his whistle with a formidable vodka/7-Up mixture, drunk straight from a plastic cup (also stolen from the Community Center basement).  After one last moment of hesitation, and another look at the deserted hallway, I let myself be persuaded:

"All right.  Cheers!"

At 9:35 a.m., vodka either wakes you or breaks you.  In my case, vodka woke me right up, at stomach-level.  Dubiously macerating with the two peanut-buttered toasts I engulfed earlier this morning, the vodka slowly coats all my gastro-intestinal organs with something like a thick mason's paste.  I try concentrating on the program J.F. still watches with a sort of transfixed perplexity, but soon all my attention spins back to the angry fermentation I can feel bubbling to the surface.  At 9:55 a.m., I can't take it anymore:

"J.F.?"

"Hmm?"

"Can we do something else?"

"M'what?"

"I don't know, get some fresh air or something…"

"What?  You're gonna barf?"

"I don't think so, but my stomach feels funny."

J.F. turns off the TV.

"Oh no…"

"What is it?"

"I feel funny too."

J.F. turns to me: he's a yellowish sort of green.  I feel like throwing up just looking at him.

"Come on.  Let's go in the gym."

I follow J.F. very carefully because each minuscule step I take sends a myriad of ripples in the deep of my abdomen.  J.F. opens garage number four and takes out a basketball.  He tries to get some action going, but his moves are leaden; he dribbles the ball like he's at death's door.   Meanwhile I let myself slide against the wall, slouching on the floor:

"No, no, don't sit down, Laurie!  It'll be worse, what with all that beer you drank last night."

Oh, that's true, I'd forgotten about that. I drank my last beer not six hours ago.

"All that's still in your system."

I feel queasy sitting down.  I get up.  J.F. tries to get one in the net.  I feel queasy standing up.  I sit back down.  J.F. looks at his basketball, which missed the net by about a quarter of a mile.  The thing rolls over to me.

"You should walk a little, Laurie.  Try taking a stroll around the gym."

"No thanks.  I don't like to walk.  Walking's to get to my car."

J.F. comes over, trailing his basketball.  He suddenly says, in a changed voice:

"Laurie, I have to tell you something…"

Just as I feared: with no advance notice, J.F. slips right into confidential mode.  He's absolutely on his own here; I'm still fully absorbed by my stomach.

"Laurie.  I cheated on Eve two days ago."

I glance over at J.F.: he's looking down at the floor now, his face a full mask of remorse.  He and Eve have been going out for more than a year. Putting a foot on his basketball, J.F. rolls it back and forth nervously before adding:

"I feel so bad.  I could just about die from guilt… Last night, I actually wept in my mother's arms, can you believe it?"

A wave of compassion overcomes me, bypassing all other consideration.  J.F. struggles, holding back obvious, genuine tears.  He looks over to me, but not quite straight on:

"You know me, Laurie.  I'm the first guy that says that a guy who cheats on his girl's a jackass.  When I hear a guy say "I couldn't help it" or "It didn't mean anything", I can't stand it.  I can't stand all that crap.  But you know what?  I *actually* felt like I couldn't help it.  I was drunk, the girl was all over me, I fucked her, period.  And it *really* felt like it didn't mean anything.  Can you believe it?  "I couldn't help it", "It didn't mean anything".  I hate myself.  I don't even know why I did it.  It wasn't even that fun, to tell you the truth.  I couldn't wait for it to be over and done with."

I don't say anything.

"You've got nothing to say?"

"I don't know…  Have you told Eve about it yet?"

"What?  No way!  I feel so terrible.  Really."

J.F. stomps around like he's trampling himself underfoot.

"And I know I'm sitting on a big pile of dynamite: she's bound to find out."

"Not if you don't tell her…"

"You think I should keep quiet about it?"

"No, I think you should be honest.  Lying's never a good idea."

"That's easy to say!  I'd like to see you in my shoes, single lady."

I smile, fully in the know:

"You're right.  I've got the gift of absolute freedom, remember?  No hassles and not being accountable to anybody."

As J.F. listens broadly, I take refuge in my own propaganda:

"The single's life is just so much simpler.  A couple's a headache."

J.F. stays silent for a moment, then he loses his serious air. He starts laughing:

"Again! Everything you just said is absolute crap! You're just trying to convince yourself that you're fine, that women don't need men, blah, blah, but you can't *wait* to be in a couple!  You're just bullshitting yourself all the way to the next guy on your list."

I blush very evenly, from ear to ear.  With my nausea dissipating, there's more room to get offended:

"Only half of it is bullshit.  The rest is true!"

J.F. laughs as he picks up his basketball:

"I see.  So you're holding out to be the part-time semi-girlfriend again?"

"If I had to choose between that and a couple, yes."

J.F. balances the ball on the back of his hand. He's smiling, relaxed now:

"Right.  You keep on telling yourself that, Laurie. I, for one, am sure you'd let Larry lead the way, all the way, in a second."

I briefly try to maintain a full onslaught of indignation, but the whole thing crumbles.  Meanwhile J.F. dribbles again, this time with a laid-back stance; he even scores without looking.

"Woo hoo!!!  Did you see that?  I'm almost at half court, too!  I'm so good, I amaze myself!"

J.F.'s tormented thoughts have a very limited shelf-life; he's already forgotten all about Eve and his own straying impromptu.  I smile in spite of myself.

Back in my fishbowl, the phone rings again.  J.F. motions to it.

"Answer it.  I'm sure it's the guy with the squirrel again."

We laugh and I let the machine pick up.

# 13

Today is P-Day. Presentation Day. Capital P, capital D, and capital headache. I got up with that this morning, with a throbbing pain taking up the entire western hemisphere of my head. It's more than a headache, it's a high-powered migraine. Every little noise hammers against my forehead. Even eating is problematic; each chew reverberates within, loudly, as I force-feed myself a breakfast of flat margarine on toast. Aside from that, I'm feeling surprisingly well. I mean, I'm not even that stressed out.

That's a bad omen.

In the train on the way over, I read my poem again, for the umpteenth time. It's just to have a clear conscience: I don't really know *how* to read it yet. I still can't figure out the beat or tone or flow. I just hope I can get it over with before the break, so I can leave afterwards. This migraine's severely depleting my reserves of energy; it's a constant battle against light, sound, the hubbub of commuters, the metal screech of the train rattling against its own volatile, clanking belly. God, my head hurts. Honestly, I'm almost glad: it's the perfect excuse to perform less than perfectly, to fail without taking responsibility. I did try to help myself, though: before leaving the house, I took two aspirins that did absolutely nothing. I even brought the whole bottle with me, but then forgot my water bottle: I need about half a gallon to down even the smallest of pills, so the whole thing's pointless anyway.

Of course, Ticket-Ticket stops to chat.

"Hello Miss Laurie!  How are you today?"

I feel like screaming "scram" right into that jolly face of his.  Poor man.  He's so full of good intentions.  I smile through my headache:

"I'm fine.  And you?"

My voice pounds against my skull, sending shockwaves of pain right through the jawbone.  Let's be honest here for a second: I said "And you?" out of pure politeness, not to start a whole conversation.  But Ticket-Ticket gets comfortable.  The train's almost empty.  He's got time on his hands:

"I'm doing great!  As always!"

His smile gets even wider.

"Off to school?"

"Yes."

"College?"

"No, university."

"My oldest son, he's in college…"

"Huh."

"…but he doesn't like it."

"Aww."

"No, instead he wants to play music with his group. Ever heard of the "Cool Dudes"?"

While I gently, cautiously shake my head no, he leans into me.

"That's the name of his group!"

"Oh."

"That's what he really likes to do.  And he's pretty good too!  When I was young, I was in a music group myself."

"Really?"

"I was the singer!"

"Is that so?"

I'm actually beginning to take an interest.

"When we started out, we used to play "skiffle". Ever heard of that?"

"Yes. I think The Beatles used to play that kind of music before…"

I almost say "before they became popular", but I cork that in. Ticket-Ticket doesn't seem to notice. He's all misty-eyed, his mustache all aflutter: streams of olden days pass through his mind.

"We called ourselves "The Grasshoppers", like Buddy Holly and his Crickets, even though it didn't sound as cool…"

I smile and let him continue.

"We had a song called "Come Back To Me". All the girls went crazy for it. We played the first few bars "tadam, toum-toum, ta-dam…". They all screamed! We'd really milk that song out, I tell you, we'd sway and wiggle and unbutton our shirts down to here."

He's pointing to the second button on his shirt, a mere three inches down from the collar.

"We were just showing off, you know, but it worked! "Come back to me, toum-toum, you're such a beau-ty-ty, ta-dam, you're the only one, toum-toum, for meeeeeee…"

I'm petrified. The few passengers that are sitting nearby all turn around and look at Ticket-Ticket as he gushes out his repertoire, using his notepad for a mike, swivelling his hips, pulling all the stops. When he finally looks down at me, staring up at him numbed with embarrassment, he laughs good-naturedly. I soon crack up too and we both chortle along.

"I'm telling you, that was our big hit!  We had so much fun in those days…"

Seeing him so moved and flooded with memories makes me feel a little melancholy myself.  I look down at my poem, sprawled on my lap.  Ticket-Ticket proudly fixes the cap on his head.

"Well, that's it for today, Miss Laurie.  Got to get back to work!"

He bows to me, comically, then walks off with a bounce in his step, checking tickets left and right.  My migraine's gone.  Just in time too; I'm getting off at the next stop.

## 14

The classroom's jam-packed. It's like everybody and the whole world came today; some people without seats even have to stand at the back of the class. A shot of panic dazes me. The teacher's not even here yet. With courage failing, I sit next to Trifocals. Normally, I try to avoid talking to him, for any and whatever purpose, including casual talk or basic pleasantries, but today the situation's too critical, regardless of expense.

"Hey?"

I don't know his name. Trifocals doesn't even look up, absorbed as he is by the third installment of Victor Hugo's *Les Misérables*:

"HEY?"

He turns around, surprised:

"Yes?"

"Why are there so many people?"

"It's an all-access day for college students. They attend a university class to see what it's like and make up their minds about applying. The teacher talked about it last week."

Last week, I was here. Physically. Mentally, I don't know. What I do know is that I didn't register that info, and now here they are: college students line every row, standing or sitting between desks or leaning against the back wall. They're easy to spot with their nonchalant air, their unconcerned expression. How I envy them.

I look down at my binder, with my poem tucked inside. It's not good enough. I can't read that! What was I thinking, writing a stupid typographic-politico-socio-geographical poem?!?  I can't read that in front of people!  God!!!  What was I thinking?!?

I jump out of my seat.  I start picking up my things, binder, pens and pencil case, flipping it all hodgepodge in my school bag.  Trifocals stares at me perplexedly, but I don't care.  As I'm grabbing my coat however, the teacher makes her entrance, smiling and enthusiastic.  She closes the door behind her.  I hesitate for a moment, then slowly, painfully, fold up my coat and sit back down again.  If I leave now, it'll be obvious, all eyes will zoom in on me, including those of the teacher, and she knows I'm scheduled for today.  I can't leave, it's too late.  Class begins:

"Hello everybody, and a very special welcome to all the college students who came here to visit us on this day of all days.  I hope you won't be disappointed!"

Everyone laughs, relaxed, while I fidget in my seat.  The teacher turns to us, her "real" students:

"Of course, our guests won't be with us for the whole class!  They'll only stay for the first half hour."

Ha!  Yes sir!  That means the teacher will give her usual feeble exposé on the many mood swings of a Jacques Prévert or a Claude Gauvreau, the college students will leave and I'll read my poem later on, after the break.  Yes, it's all falling into place now.  Poems are always read right after the break.  I'd forgotten that.  Yes, that's right!  Phew!  That was close!  Once again, I worried myself sick over nothing: I'll just read my poem after the break.  All's well.

I audaciously breathe in and out while the teacher opens her leather briefcase and takes out her notebook.  She addresses the visiting students again:

"To get us into the spirit of things, I always start my class with a presentation on a specific poet, his or her working methods, the complexity of his or her compositions, and his or her many moods."

I knew it. All's well, all's well.

"But this morning, we'll do things backwards. We'll start with what my students and I always keep for the second half of our class: the reading of original poems."

I keep on smiling like a moron because I'm not sure I heard her right.

"I'm very proud of my students, and it's with the greatest of pleasures that I invite you to sample some of their creations."

Now I heard her. I feel weird, like I'm having an out-of-body experience, but in-the-body. It's never happened this intensely to me before, feeling at once this connected and disconnected, getting numb all over, with things blurring, sounds dislocating, and my heart beating on an off-beat, like outside itself. God! I can't believe this! At the back of the class, visitors smile, distractingly thinking "Original poems, should be interesting...", while ordinary students slouch back in their chairs, feeling comfortably spared. Shitting hell!

"Well, let's start. First, I must ask you to please keep quiet during a reading. It's very important, out of respect for the student doing the presentation..."

The teacher looks at her notebook again.

"Now, now, let's see... The first person to read this morning is... where's my list? Ah! Here it is! Laurie."

She looks up and stares at me confidently.

"Laurie?  You're up!  We're all listening."

I take out my poem, barely conscious of the fact. In the next few seconds, empty silence almost suffocates me; I want to start, but no words come out.  In reality, I mean in real life, the delay must seem like a temporary lapse, a brief pause, a few moments of quickly forgiven vacillation, but in my desperate private universe, it's an endless stretch of time that grows and swells and brings all possible anxiety levels to a maximum.

I read the title:

"There's No Fucking Place like Home"

I don't stop to see or hear if there's a reaction in the classroom.  I'm too scared.  All my desperation at the thought of being here now, at having to read in front of people I don't know, of being forced to share something intimate, all my fears of failing, all my rage against the university machine, of its misuse of our talents and dreams, its useless degrees and diplomas, landing us on the job market with no hopes whatsoever of a job worthy of the name, all that pours into my voice as I go on reading:

"From far and wide
Looking safe from outside
Stable, easy, almost perfect
But in time, here's the verdict:
 Suburbs kill
God-awful West Island
Amputated isle
Waterways by the mile
Stuck drably in the middle
Six or seven towns gone local
Exiled by flower contests

Or bans on social protests
God-awful West Island
With its calculated trees
Lining private alleys
Big empty houses
Standing tall on their courses
God-awful West Island
Shrinking woodlands and forests
For tidy parks and florists
Shopping malls and dentists
God-awful West Island
I wish you'd fall off the deep end."


I stuttered a little, with words slightly slowed and suspended by my initial resistance, but even though I accelerated too much on the last few verses, I'm done! That's it! It's over and done with! I've read my poem!

That's when it hits me. There's nothing in the classroom. Not a sound. My voice died down, it dwindled and faded in a vacuum of prolonged silence. Even now, no one says anything. Way in the back, a guy shuffles his feet; his soles squeak. That's it. That's the only sound. I look at the teacher, eyes wide on her like a last cry for help. She turns away and looks at the other students:

"Any comments?"

More shuffling, some movement and a little cough. Nothing. Not one word. The teacher steps in:

"Well, I'll make a comment. First, notice how Laurie has what I call a fist-first type of writing. It's all about revolt. It's blunt, the rhythm is hard, almost violent. It almost reads like a military march. What I like about this poem is the beat, very syncopated, punctuated. It's very catchy.  What I like less, of course, is the use of a crude word like "fucking", in the title.  That's too obvious. I wonder if that's really necessary.  It feels like overkill, maybe, but I'm guessing it's representative of Laurie's feelings of isolation in her social environment."

My fist-first writing?  My feelings of isolation?

One of my peers raises her hand:
"I think the whole "suburbia angst" angle has been done to death."
Another hand:
"It's been done to death because it's still true."
"Yeah but we've heard all that a thousand times before already."
"I'm not even sure what the West Island is."
"It's a suburb."
"No, it's a collection of rich, pretentious suburbs. Which is why it's worth denouncing."
As the polemic continues, I say nothing and listen less.  After five minutes, my poem is no longer mine.  The group is taking it apart, analysing it point by point, discussing theories on residential paranoia and the constipated idiosyncrasies of the bourgeois.  I'm out of my depth.
The girl who raised her hand first raises it again, this time speaking to me directly:
"I think the rhyme "houses/courses" is very feeble."
Everybody turns to me.  I quickly look down at my poem, at the two accused verses:
"Yes, that's… that's regrettable."

Instantly, the whole class bursts out laughing.  The bonhomie of my answer completely defused the tension.  I look around, a little surprised at first, but then I laugh as well, relieved.  Even the teacher giggles and takes the opportunity to sell her class to the college students, all of whom are giggling with her unanimously:

"You see?  What matters here is not to discourage the student but to help him, or her, revisit his or her poem, to write it again, to throw new light on it.  Well done, Laurie.  Thank you for this beautiful offering.  Sylvester, it's your turn now."

While the guy called Sylvester reads his poem, I'm everything except attentive.  It's insane how good I feel, it's like I'm invincible.  After their half hour with us, the college students leave.  As do I, after the break.

15

Today, I've decided to take a break from life. I woke up, as usual, with the heinous sound of the buzzer from my alarm clock (I tried setting it on "radio" to wake up to music instead, but it doesn't work: the music becomes part of my dream and I never wake up). So I got up, ate breakfast, both eyes swimming in my cereals, got to Beaconsfield, eyes still unfocused – and then made a decision. I was looking at the train station, with its frayed walls and dirty windows, when I suddenly thought "No, not this morning. I'm not putting myself through that again. This morning, screw school, I'm going back to bed". Ah....... I turned around and headed back home, smiling only slightly because I felt guilty, looking at the other commuters. Alone in my car I got over it, though, and sang all the way home. Ah....... If only people could do something like that every once in a while, if only we all could say "You know what, today I'm not up to it", and stay home. I went to bed and slept another two, three hours. My bed was still warm. I told myself I deserved it, what with my poem presentation this week. I must reward myself for my efforts. I've been on edge for so long, I owe it to myself.

I'm busy reading a comic book when the phone rings. Argh... I don't feel like talking. On the sixth ring, I reluctantly pick up:

"Hello?"

"Err... May I speak to Laurie please?"

"Speaking."

"Laurie?"

"Yes?"

"It's Miguel."

It takes me a few seconds to assemble voice, name and face in my mind. Miguel: Sharon's ex, Maude's pal… and one of Larry's best friends.

"Miguel?"

"Yeah, err… Sorry to bother you, but… I just wanted to say it was fun seeing you again at the beer bash…"

I answer very slowly, out of utter perplexity.

"Yes. Thank you. It was fun seeing you too."

"Err, I just wanted to know if we could go see a movie or something, tonight or sometime…"

"A movie? But I thought Guss didn't want to see anybody anymore: he says he's been shortchanged on bad dope at the bash. I mean, he's the one who's got everyone's number. So, if he's not coming…"

Miguel interrupts me:

"Err… no. I meant, just you and me."

It's like the sentence doesn't correlate with Miguel's status in my life. All I can think of, is that he's Sharon's old boyfriend. Sharon and Miguel dated for six months six years ago. Their whole relationship was mostly sinless and ended with a flow of unjustified recriminations from both parties. That's too bad; they made a nice, very aesthetic couple. Anyway, from what I've seen back at the bash, the passage of years have left Miguel unchanged, with time having no effect on him, either good or bad: he still has that determined profile, his eyes perpetually glowering, advertising his willful and difficult temper. He's extremely handsome, in a given sort of way, but he leaves me cold. I prefer ugly guys with panache. I need a little extra charm, sex-appeal, mystery – a little something that Miguel does not have. And it *would* be a bad trick to play on Sharon for me to go out, even chastely, with her ex. So after a brief survey of my emotions, I know I'm not interested. Nevertheless, I must exercise diplomacy.

While I'm still thinking, Miguel fills my silence:

"We don't have to go see a movie, I mean, we can do something else, like go somewhere, like, I don't know, I've heard Larry and Guss talking about a GT…"

My heart gives a lurch; Larry's name instantly fires me up. A GT is a "get-together", an umbrella expression that includes any and all activities performed as a group and consisting mostly of getting drunk, stoned, or drunk and stoned again. Since Larry was mentioned, I delicately mould my answer:

"That's great, Miguel, but I guess a GT means all the other girls will be present as well: Cyn, Maude, Nicky… and Sharon?"

"Err, yeah, I guess…"

"Don't you think it would be a little weird if the two of us showed up together? I mean with Sharon being your ex and all…"

"Well, if we go to the movies, just the two of us, no one has to know about it…"

I see I wasn't clear enough. I try again:

"That's nice of you Miguel, but I don't think it's a good idea. When's the GT, by the way?"

I hope my "no thanks" was understood but eased out by my question. It works. Miguel answers, seemingly unfazed:

"Guss said he'll call you about it."

"Perfect."
"…"
"So we'll see each other there, then?"
"Err, okay.  Bye."
"Bye."

I hang up.  Poor Miguel.  Towards the end there, he sounded a little disappointed.

I hotline the whole thing back to Nicky, to tell her about this supposedly upcoming GT.  Ever since her epoch-making conversation with Cedric, Nicky has been feeling rather blue, with a daily dose of bitter brooding further eroding her already endangered lust for life.  On the way back from the beer bash, she told me all about her big moment with Cedric: in keeping with her incisive nature, Nicky skipped the pleasantries and landed on him with a loud and clear "We need to talk".  Feeling cornered, Cedric immediately switched to self-defence mode, adopting the stare, stance and stature of complete couldn't-care-less-ness.  Undeterred, Nicky plowed on, saying she wanted to spend more time with him.  Cedric reacted to this by saying nothing and widening his eyes.  Nicky's straightforwardness itself came out of fear; she only wanted to get an answer as fast as possible to get the thing over and done with as fast as possible.  But when she asked Cedric point-blank "Are you interested?" what she finally got was a long speech about Maude.  Professing his undying friendship for one-third of their threesome, Cedric talked about being "real friends", about things he felt "deep down" and the impossibility of "double-crossing Maude or whatever".  Nicky got fed up real fast; he was still talking when she left him there.  Since that night, Nicky came out of seclusion twice: once to buy beer, once to buy painkillers.  Things are that bad.  What's more, Cyn phoned to tell us that Cedric rounded off the beer bash by smooching in a corner with Loni Bouchard…  So that's that.

When I tell Nicky about Miguel's own endeavour towards me, she jumps:

"He's Sharon's ex!"

"I know."

"Let's hope you're not getting *that* desperate."

"Let's."

As expected, Nicky's less than enthusiastic about the GT.

"And for the GT, no thanks.  I don't want to see those guys anymore.  I really don't."

"I know."

"And you.  You only want to go there to see Larry again."

I almost fall back on denying the whole thing, but it's useless:

"Yeah, I still want to see him."

"Be careful, Laurie; Larry was never sure of anything in his life.  No one can tell what he thinks about anything.  As for Miguel, stay *way* away from him.  I'm sure it would hurt Sharon if she found out."

"Oh, don't worry about him.  He's off the radar. I'll just let things lie.  Anyway, Guss still hasn't called, so…  Maybe the whole thing's off."

"Well I'm not going in any case."

"That's too bad.  I'd need the support."

"You're really gonna go?"

I think for a moment.  My options: follow Nicky's advice, and the voice of reason, and stay home, or try my luck again.  Nicky gets impatient:

"Well?"

"I'll go by myself."

## 16

Unsurprisingly, Guss hasn't called yet. Miguel never called back either, which is just as well. Also worrying me are midterm papers. Next week at the latest, I'll have to actually sit down and put pen to paper if I don't want to get even more stretched out, stress-wise. Since I read my poem in class, I was left hanging by the teacher; no grades are out yet, so I'm not sure how to write that 15-page essay she wants. Did she like my style? Should I write differently? What's the angle? I have no idea how to go about it. It's making me so nervous, I think about it at night instead of sleeping. No wonder. Slaving at university-level takes a heavy toll: whenever I *do* sleep, I dream in literary form, my thoughts classified, codified and systematized, with hook, thesis and outline all arranged and positioned while my mind swirls between content and context. That's what I get after all those years of writing for school, hoping to get good grades. That's how it works: nice intelligent words = candy. Not every teacher is duped of course, but generally speaking, playing the part of the cultivated smart-ass is an academic pandemic.

That's exactly what happened to one of our friends, Edith. Edith was a nice girl; we knew her from elementary school, Nicky and I. She started a bachelor's degree in Music and then one day, it happened: she was abducted. It happened just like that, pfuit!, we didn't even see her go. When we realized she had deserted and joined ranks with the smart-asses, it was already too late; she was fully roped in, organizing "symphonic meetings" at the cultural center near her house. She even invited me once, explaining "You, Laurie, are a real artist, and I only invite true, genuine artists" before adding that she permitted Nicky to tag along, as a grand courtesy to me. Needless to say, I was a little disconcerted, especially considering the fact that I am definitely not an artist (unless an artist is someone who can't find a real job). Anyway, Nicky and I decided to go, just for laughs. When we got there, arriving merrily with our six-pack of beer, we knew right away it was a mistake. First of all, everybody there was dressed in black – but not because it looks nice or because it's comfortable. No, I mean dressed in black as in with black frills, black lace, black jabots, scarfs and berets – the whole parade of paraphernalia worn just to look interesting. Second of all, everybody was drinking wine from tall, limited-edition wine glasses. When Nicky and I drink wine, it's from the bottle through a straw. Third of all, the whole atmosphere was suffocating because everyone was so ridiculously serious. It's hard to laugh and have fun when people are "intense".

Always a gracious hostess, Edith made every effort to greet Nicky and I cordially, but she was more embarrassed by our presence among her new friends than happy to make introductions. Now, Nicky and I have known each other for a long time, and I knew, after that cold one-second glance she shot me, that we'd be leaving in less than fifteen minutes. While we tried to come up with plausible excuses so we could exit without being impolite, real artists suddenly took center stage, playing charades with the Great Classics. That could've been fun to watch, except that the game immediately got bogged down by players trying to flaunt their knowledge. As we all know, extended knowledge takes up a lot of space. It's hard to laugh and have fun when people claw and gnaw to scream "Prokofiev!" before everybody else. When we got up to leave, Nicky and I, Edith came up and said "You're leaving already?" but she looked relieved. Getting home with our six-pack intact, Nicky and I thought about it and came up with our own conclusion: culture never made anyone intelligent.

Integrity is such a rare thing in school. At the end of my first week in Literature, I ended up back at Nicky's apartment, crying my eyes out. She still remembers it. After two bloody caesars, I burst into tears, big shaking sobs – the kind you have to let out before you can talk again. I thought everybody fitted and belonged, except me. I felt I was the only one who resented how students were expected to prostrate and genuflect to the gods of the learned: assimilate, repeat and shut up. I was so sad, so disappointed.

Even now, three years later, I can't take it. Even now, as I sit in my Dramatic Writing class, I'm as anxious as ever. I'm waiting for a grade here as well. It's for a 10-page description of the narrative thread of the play I'm supposed to write, later in the term. This time, I chose to stop playing the dutiful student and used my "true" voice instead, warts and all. I don't know yet if my audacity paid off.

With fifteen minutes to go before the break, the professor – that self-copulating twit with the rainbow colored sweater-vests – finally wraps up his homily on Ionesco. He then prepares to hand us back our papers, which he corrected over the weekend. Swallowing hard under his bow tie, he glares at us through the piles of essays languishing on his desk:

"Now please listen to me, carefully: I *know* what your work is worth…"

With the back of his hand, he nonchalantly brushes away a few essays from the first pile, some of which fall to the ground. In our classroom, two or three students cough a little nervously. The professor goes on, his voice prophet-like:

"Your subjects are unprepossessing, for the most part, and the few among you who were able to find a topic worthy of interest, treated it amateurishly. I am deeply, deeply concerned…"

From the great heights of his plentiful erudition, the professor slowly wipes his brow, his hand heavy with lassitude. Then it happens. The moment is solemn, consecrated by an unprecedented feeling of importance among us, the students: for the first time since classes began, the professor gets up from behind his desk. For the first time in seven weeks, the bottom half of his body appears to us in all its glorious splendor. I can't help but observe, along with everybody else, the extent of the damage: patent-leather white shoes open on brown socks that run up the legs to junction the pants, a part-pinkish part-velvet disaster of bulky breeches that relent just below the knee. I honestly can't believe it. Behind me, two students chuckle. With a superhuman effort, I manage to keep a straight face while the professor looks at me, for some reason. Thankfully, he soon moves on, blabbering away, hoping to get us to nod along pensively instead of staring at him bemusedly. With a regal air, he slowly bends over and picks up the papers that fell on the floor a moment ago:

"When you write your play, later this term, always keep in mind the comments, remarks and directions I wrote here, in the margins of your preparatory essays."

With that, he turns and heads back to his desk, where he sits down again. He starts calling us by name, one by one, to give us our papers back. Of course, all the students get nervous. The professor takes full advantage of the opportunity: he asks us to read, out loud, the basic plot of our plays so he may comment on it for the benefit of the whole class.

The first wave of executions follows. About five or six students go through this ordeal, being forced to stand there, copy in trembling hand, baring their all and then getting dissected for everyone to see. Only one person clearly enjoys this: the professor, who not only listens but also shows us *how much* he's listening. Sitting there, apparently deep in concentration, his mental digestion magnified, he looks on with his hands pressed one against the other, in a rigid triangle. Not content to simply display this fixed effort, he insists on explaining at length, to each and every student, the general terms of his correction, which are already written in the margins, as he himself pointed out. A painful exercise, first and foremost for the student being publicly post-mortemed, and then ultimately for other students enduring the long walk-through leading up to their own immolation.

After a few minutes, it's my turn. When the professor calls my name, I get up, already aching with dread, and walk over to his desk, extending my hand to recuperate my work. The professor looks at me, his eyes hard above the document.  From my vantage point, I can clearly see the spatters of red ink that maculate my cover page; comments, remarks and directions.  I keep my hand out, still fully extended, hoping this will somehow accelerate the process.  Bad idea.  The professor zeroes in on me with renewed intensity, his blazing eyes scanning my face like a gaping microscope.  A heavy lead-like silence paralyses the other students; like me, they await the terrible fall of the guillotine.  It's funny, but from where I'm standing, I notice a little thread that's come undone in the professor's bow tie.  And then, at last, it begins.

The next moment, I'm still trying to make sense of what just happened.  When the professor opened his mouth, out came a shrill "Ah hahhhhhhhhhhhhhh!" that completely took me by surprise and made everybody else sit up in a collective question mark.  Bearing the full brunt of the assault, I remain perfectly still, shocked into immobility.  The professor brandishes my copy, which he willfully points to, shaking it towards the rest of the class:

"Dear friends, what you see here is Laurie's essay – an excellent example of everything that is wrong with your own work, but thrown into one single potpourri of intolerable malapropisms."

I think I'm about to faint.  Struggling to keep my balance, I look on as the professor, now on a roll, perfects his critique:

"The setting is not bad: an afternoon spent in a suburban Community Center."

I know, I know – but I didn't know what to write about.  Back at work, J.F. told me I should write a play about us and our customer service issues.  I actually thought it might actually be funny.

The professor looks down at my cover page again, with the endless streaks of red notes splashed everywhere. My heart is pounding in my throat. With eyes slowly panning across the classroom, he points to my essay again:

"Narrow-minded, overflowing with primitive, unidimensional characters, with no central structure and a linear narrative that all but disintegrates upon close examination."

My eyes water.

The professor dumps my essay on his desk. That's when I see my grade: C-. Another. For the first time, the professor turns to me and smiles. It's a warm, enveloping smile, offered like some sort of refuge against the hellish public trauma I'm being subjected to. Then, out of the blue, he takes my hand in his and squeezes it comfortingly for a few seconds. After all, it's his job, his duty even, to criticize my work so that I may improve and grow out of my own limitations. Yes. He's trying to help me.

I bravely choke back the tears. The professor etches a smile again. When he finally hands me back my essay, he adds, with a genteel air of disdain:

"It's televisual."

With my hands folded over my paper, tightly pressed against my chest, I head back to my seat, hoping the students' single converging eye will soon detach from me. Not to worry: the girl who follows me has it even worse. The professor makes her write out her play's entire dramatic arc on the blackboard, like a second grader. The poor girl shook like a leaf the whole time.

When he's finally done handing out our papers, the professor bombards us with "hints" and "pointers" again. Gulping importantly through his bow tie, he says:

"There is no subjectivity without distance: write that down."

While everyone docilely complies, scribbling in unison, I also bend over my notebook, writing a series of expletives with a conscientious grin. The professor's still not done picking at us. With a manicured index, he points to another victim: a guy sitting deep in his seat, wearing an old heavy metal T-shirt:

"You there, in the back!"

The guy in question jumps up and nervously slicks back his straggling locks, pointing to himself timidly. The professor hauls him in:

"Yes, yes, you. Tell us: does temporality affect the proscenium?"

I know it's not nice, but seeing the guy's face decompose bit by bit because he, quite obviously, can't answer the question, consoles me a little for what happened earlier on. This guy, by now literally white from panic, tries to concoct the semblance of a coherent sentence, all the while hiding behind the students in front of him, and, if possible, those on each side. With a heavy sigh, the professor waves him off and instead turns to his favorite student, a young bald philosopher-type with a goatee:

"Temporality, sir, affects the proscenium insofar as the play itself allows for its own density to act as a unifying force."

"Yes, Julian, very good. But you might also add that this density only drives the play when it transcends that very unity."

"Very well said, sir."

On the way home, I read the professor's red notes on my essay. He's right. I should stop writing. Period. I should never write again. Not one word. After all, I've got nothing to say, really. Nothing of importance, whether in a play, or a poem, or in my life in general. It's true: I am televisual. I'm in the normal norm, leading a life that doesn't bother anyone, that doesn't matter anyway. I'm not special. Yes, a few harsh words from a little professor in buffoon pants, and there it is: self-loathing. He's right in part, though. I think I've lost something through the years. I've become too reliable, stable, predictable, reasonable. I wonder if the professor would prefer that concept. Sure he would.

## 17

I can't stop writing.  I *have* to work on my midterms: four essays in total, and less days left before the deadline than pages to hand in.  I sit down in our study, facing a pile of mandatory reference books and a stack of sheets I bought yesterday, on sale and in bulk.  I take out a pen.  Fifteen minutes later, I'm still sitting in the same position; the end of my pencil has been masticated and there's a wobbly stick figure on the sheet in front of me.  I haven't opened a book yet.

Okay.  Instead of goofing off all afternoon, I'll draw up an informal balance sheet, just to sort my thoughts out:

<u>What really sucks</u>:

a) Sleep: I can't sleep because of migraines, which gives me more migraines.

b) School: writing for school has become synonymous with constantly dishing out a flat series of all-purpose approximations.  Yes, I've become a master in the art of killing content through form.

c) School again: I'm required by class regulations to read idiotic but essential books to cross-reference all those essays I have to write, all this just to tack on a nice, plush, annotated bibliography rearwards.

d) My car: it's old.  I have to drive with the radio at top volume at all times so I don't hear all those crazy sounds it's making.  Also, the ignition key's loose: driving around with one hand constantly plugging it in is a little dangerous.

e) Time and money: never have enough of either to get properly, mind-blowingly wasted –although I could make arrangements.

f) Larry, Larry, Larry.

g) Life: everybody looks like they know what their life's purpose is, except me.

I think I'd better stop right here, or else I'll get even more depressed. If I really put my mind to it, I'm sure I can find other things – positive things – to cheer myself up. I draw up another list:

<u>What sucks less:</u>

a) Midterm means no classes for a week.
b) My car still works.

I know. This list is shorter, but it took me twice as long to put it to paper. It's not my fault if I keep confusing realism and pessimism. I'm always thinking the worst thing that could happen will happen because the opposite would be too good to be true. Like at the Community Center: in the winter, I have to cross the skating rink (on boots, not skates) to move the nets out of the way for the Zamboni driver. Then I have to shovel the snow he makes when he drives off. Every time I step on that rink, I can see myself falling face first on the ice, breaking all my front teeth. My imagination is so vivid, I can feel everything: the broken teeth that clink together, sawing through my lips, filling my mouth with a warm flow of blood.  When I try to scream to the Zamboni driver that I've had an accident, all my teeth give way, dangling from a ripped thread of gums.  Disgusting.  And I keep thinking about it!  Because I'm convinced that one day, all this will happen, it's an absolute certainty.

I look at the stack of sheets in front of me again. Maybe I should start with the play for my Dramatic Writing class.  At least those C minuses I got showed me I can still nearly flunk out, even this close to graduation. Teachers never get how important a grade is.  They're never fully aware of how much it all matters. Bad grades have a lot of side-effects.  Good grades don't count. Quickly forgotten, they're practically of no consequence, but a bad grade can render a student inoperative for a few days, it can even cause unduly anticipation of other essays or exams, or increase stress for other grades in other classes. Even an absent grade can cause damage. Case in point: my Poetry class.  The teacher still hasn't graded my poem on the West Island.  What's she waiting for?  I can't write all those other poems she wants without knowing what she thinks of the first one first.  The whole thing makes no sense.  If only I could just drop out right here, right now...  There's only, what, eight weeks left before graduation?  And then what?  I don't even know what to do next, how to get out of the quagmire and find work – supposing that finding work means getting out of the quagmire...

Well, that's it.  There's no writing to be done today. Leaving papers and books behind, I drive down, hand to ignition, to the student placement center, like Nicky said I should.  All in good faith.  The center itself is a large room with a lot of shelves, like a library.  A dry musty smell permeates the whole place, immediately bunging up my throat.  It's either that or the stress of just being here.  I swallow sideways and approach the receptionist, a woman in her thirties with interminable fingernails.  She's busy crossing out names on a list, drawing a long line over every name with a ruler.  For a moment, I wonder if all those names belong to Literature students who were unable to find work after graduating.  Not wanting to interrupt, I wait for her to finish.  When she reaches the bottom of the page, she looks up at me and smiles:

"Yes?"

"I would like to know if you can help me…"

She doesn't say anything but her smile congeals. She doesn't look like she wants to help me.  I venture anyway:

"I'm graduating this year, in Literature…"

I don't finish; another woman, an older one, emerges from behind a shelf.  The two now exchange a worried look.  The youngest of the pair looks at me again:

"Yes, how may I help you?"

I hesitate while the older woman leans in.  My clammy hands smudge the edge of the counter to which I'm desperately clinging to:

"I'd just like to know if you can help me find a job in my field…"

The two women look at each other again, dismayed; the eldest motions to the other with a flick of the chin.  The gesture was meant to go undetected but I've spotted the get-rid-of attitude in her huff.  The young receptionist replies confidently:

"You can look through our network. Jobs in your field will be listed. It's right through there, near the entrance."

From here, I can see the place she's pointing to: it's a small and deserted cubicle-like space, with three old computers squatting in a row. Two of them look disabled. The third one is loudly humming.

"Thank you. I'll do that."

The two women look on as I enter the cubbyhole. Satisfied, they both resume work after heaving a very audible sigh of relief.

The computer facing me now roars malevolently. The keyboard shakes from the vibration. Or is it my trembling hands? I type in "literature". The computer makes a weird little sound, like a gnashing rumble, happy to wake up, to be of use. The answer comes up quickly on the screen. The blinking cursor spells out the words "no available results". A little surprised, I frown for a moment, then type in "Literature", with a capital "L". Little rumble. The answer pops up: "two options". I click on the first option. The screen goes blank, with no cursor anywhere on the page. For a few seconds, a wayward sort of guilt overcomes me as I contemplate the fact that I might have single-digitally killed the computer. Suddenly however, a whole page of text appears. I read the title: "Professor – College Level". Yuck. I skip the description and go back to the previous page. I open the second option. The screen goes blank again, but I remain calm. Soon, another page of text appears. The title: "Professor – University Level". Double yuck.

I go back to the start-up page. I type in "Literature" again. The computer makes a gut-deep rattle like it's rebelling against my obstinateness. It answers: "two options".

Demoralized, I look over and beyond the monitor: the two women are talking in a low voice, glancing at me at intervals. I get up and leave. As I make my exit, I feel like I've just narrowly escaped with my life, somehow.

When I get home, I call Nicky to blow off some steam. The line's busy. As soon as I hang up, the phone rings.

"Laurie? Hi, it's Guss. What's up?"

"Guss? Oh, hi. How are you?"

"Doing okay. Are you busy?"

"No, no."

"Ah... You know, I wanted to tell you: back at the beer bash, I acted like a jerk. I got pissed off at everybody over nothing."

"Yeah, you know, it happens..."

"Anyway, sorry about that..."

"It's okay. I'm sorry too, if I hurt your feelings in any way."

"Yeah, well... Hey! There's a GT in two weeks, did you know?"

"I know, Miguel told me."

"Miguel? How come?"

Oops. I stepped right into that one. Guss' indignant curiosity comes to an instant boil. I try to salvage the situation:

"Yeah, he called because he wanted to know if anyone had found his glasses... He lost them at the bash."

I know: this is a terrible, pitifully lame, eye-poking obvious lie. At the other end of the line, Guss stays silent. I know he's weighing each and every word, busy evaluating probabilities and eventualities.  I change the subject:

"So where's the GT at?"

Guss answers, his still-pleasant tone sounding like a peace offering:

"We don't know yet, but everybody'll be there. Are you and Nicky coming?"

"I'm not sure.  I don't think Nicky's up to it.  She's got a lot of homework."

Another lie.  Even though he detects the defects in my voice, Guss plows on:

"What about you?  Are you coming?"

"I don't know yet.  Call me back when you know where it'll be."

"Right.  It's in two weeks, remember."

"I won't forget, Guss.  Thanks.  Bye."

"Bye."

All right, so that's settled: the GT, with Larry in perspective, is in two weeks.  I know I should try and preserve what little dignity I have left, I know I should listen to my inner voice and bow down to the fact that seeing Larry again is not, is never, a good idea – but I still feel torn.  I'll think about it later.  I'll decide then.

## 18

During the midterm break, I went to Vermont with Nicky, for three days.  I hurried and finished writing all my essays, and we decamped, Nicky and I, for the express purpose of seeing if we can still out-trip ourselves in spite of our venerable old age.  While Nicky smokes up a storm on the drive over, I look forward to getting to that chalet we rented.  I also concentrate on the road ahead; the long straight highways of Montreal and their congested bridges, the dull flatness of farms, cows and silos in the Eastern Townships, the fun of getting through customs without looking like we're holding, the view on Lake Champlain, the growing Appalachian mountain range and, finally, Vermont itself, as such.

Vermont is green.  It's nice, but it's mostly flaming green, full of rolling green mountains.  I prefer Montreal.

After our arrival, Nicky and I quickly bore-out.  It's always raining so we watch television.  On the third morning, Nicky tries to boost our morale.  After spending the last two days sprawled on the sofa with the ashtray on her tummy, she raises herself slightly, leaning on an elbow:

"Hey Laurie?  Maybe we should go for a drive…"

"What?  What for?"

"I don't know.  We should go and see the mountains or something."

"I can see them from here: they're green."

I don't like to travel (for me, going to Vermont is travelling; I never leave the island except to go sugar-shacking every other decade).  My lack of enthusiasm doesn't bother Nicky too much, though: we're both following the path of least possible effort. Our last two lunches consisted in four bags of chips. For dinner, we reheated a couple of hot dogs, without the bun.

I just woke up. I slept in the living room because I couldn't muster enough willpower to climb up the stairs to get to my bedroom. I don't like the beds here, anyway. They smell like hospital beds.

"What time is it?"

Nicky turns on her right side to face me. She answers:

"Nine o'clock."

"In the morning?"

She lights a cigarette.

"No, in the afternoon."

Nicky's sarcastic tone is habitual in the early hours. She's not a morning person. We both know we should avoid contact for at least thirty minutes after bestirring ourselves, but today neither one of us has the necessary drive to get up and leave the room. I revert to watching TV, with the sound off. Nicky drops her next sentence through a sigh:

"So? Still thinking of going to the GT?"

"Yes."

"Shit. Why? Why in the world would you want to put yourself through that again?"

I offer no answer.

"You really think you can still pull in Larry?"

The pseudo-interrogation's starting to get on my nerves: I'm trying to watch a commercial.

"When you say it like that, it sounds like it's a bad idea."

"It *is* a bad idea."

Nicky draws on her smoke, one eye half-shut.

"Listen Laurie, you're free to do as you please. But don't come crying to me when it all conks out."

The commercial's getting on my nerves too. I fidget on the sofa, trying to find the remote. Nicky goes on:

"Forget about Larry, will you? You've been at it for two years already and you've made no progress whatsoever."

What makes her comment even worse, is her tone: it has softened. The empathy's deafening, humiliating. I exhale, feeling exhausted all of a sudden: there's no remote in my sofa.

"Do you have the remote? I'm tired of watching this."

"If only you'd move on or something..."

"Nicky! The remote!"

Flipping on her left side, Nicky sticks one hand behind her back and pulls out the remote from God knows where. Grabbing the thing from her, I'm soon clicking all over the dial with a practiced hand. Nicky buries herself in her sofa again but she looks at me head on.

"Laurie, listen to me: it's never gonna happen."

"You don't know that."

"Yes I do. And you know it too."

Nicky said this with so much compassion, so much calm certainty, the notion gains on me. I turn to face her.

"You really think he's not interested?"

"Yes. And I know you'll waste your time trying to change that. Then you'll call me, you'll want us to analyze this and that, all the little details of his behavior: "He looked at me this way", "He said this that way"… It just makes me angry to see you waste so much time and energy on a guy who's not even worth two cents. He's not worth it. There. You deserve much better."

"I was just hoping that this time, it would be different, that's all."

"Different how? He weaseled out that time when he made you think you were gonna sleep together and nothing happened. You can't trust the guy, remember?"

"Yeah."

"He's a pussy-teaser..."

We giggle.

"You're right, you're right. It's just that it's difficult being alone all the time. I might as well apply to a convent and become a nun."

Nicky laughs:

"Come on. Why don't you just find someone else?"

"Okay. Where do you want me to find someone else?"

Nicky giggles again.

"Why don't you try your luck with Gamache?"

I look at Nicky in disbelief. Gamache is, by far, the heaviest guy in the gang, with heaviest to be taken in every sense of the word: three hundred pounds of red hair, tattoos, bad ideas and cocaine. He could be menacing in a nice sort of way, but Gamache is also the kind of guy who braids his hair delicately and drives his motorcycle with crocodile boots and a leopard-skin coat. He's a weird tough guy/corny guy mix. I get nauseous just thinking about him:

"Gamache. Are you kidding?"

Nicky laughs again. She *is* kidding. I squint back at the TV set, but my interest's waning.

"Why don't you just stay home, Laurie? Skip that GT, you'll be better off."

"...I still feel like going."

Nicky turns to me. She shakes her head, smiling:

"So pigheaded..."

I smile.

"I just want to get to the bottom of things."

Nicky chortles at my feeble double entendre. She then squashes her cigarette in the ashtray, gets up and walks over to her knapsack, which she left near the front door. She takes out a comb. Bending forward, she proceeds to untangle her wild mane methodically.

"I always start underneath. Otherwise my hair gets knotty."

I distractingly click the remote again. There's another commercial. This time they're selling "disposable containers". Nicky flings her head back, making her hair billow around her.

"Hey, Laurie. Do you remember all those hair phases I had? At eight years old, I had the greaser phase: short with a pompadour on top and two curly things on each side."

"Ha! Ha! I remember! You looked like you had two sideburns!"

"'Can't believe my mom let me go out like that! After that, I had my porcupine phase."

"Ah, yes. Spiked on top! I think everybody had that phase at one point."

"Then there was the doggy phase, with a cocker spaniel perm."

I laugh, reminiscing.

"Oh yeah!  I'd forgotten about that.  Oh my…  I like you better now."

Nicky smiles and puts her comb back in her knapsack. Then she says, quite suddenly:

"Damn that Cedric.  What a loser..."

I look at her.  Smile gone now, she hangs her head, her brow furrowed.

"Yeah but Nicky, you intimidated him."

With a little indignant air, Nicky considers me incredulously.

"Intimidated?  Cedric?  No way.  He's just stupid. I've never been so turned off in my life.  I really thought there was something between us, you know.  I can't believe he's that squeamish.  Big fat dud."

"Come on, Nicky, you know better. You know you have to let a guy think he's making the first move.  He has to think he's holding the thick stick…"

Nicky laughs at me:

"You mean "the thick end of the stick"."

"Whatever.  You know what I mean.  You just completely castrated the poor guy."

I point to the commercial:

"That's what you need.  A "disposable boyfriend": an inflatable specimen you can shove back in the drawer when you're done using it."

Nicky smiles and lights another cigarette; her tone is grave again.

"Look at what happened to me, Laurie.  I don't want that to happen to you. You don't want to see Larry trying to slime his way out of telling you he's not interested."

I nod half-heartedly.

"I guess not."

"Right.  So just forget the whole thing."

"Maybe you're right."

"I'm telling you.  I'm being serious here.  You already know what his answer's gonna be."

Next day, I decide to go to the GT anyway. Nicky's disappointed but not surprised; she respects my decision.  After three days spent watching TV, eating chips, drinking beer and staying almost perfectly still, we pack up and drive back to Canada.  On the way up, I feel a tinge of guilt:

"Nicky?  Weren't we supposed to go tripping in Vermont?"

"Yeah but it rained."

"Oh, that's right.  I forgot, it rained.  That's why we didn't do anything."

"That's it."

We mutually agree: if the weather had been nicer, we would've gone kayaking, horse-riding, hiking, the whole thing.

19

Back in Montreal, I give my four essays a final once-over. Not too bad. I'm even looking forward to handing them in: it makes graduation feel that much closer. It's sad, but writing like that, forced, for school, really takes a lot out of me. It's like going back to class; it felt so good, being on vacation, even a dull green vacation in Vermont. Beats going to school any day.

My first class this week is Poetry. The teacher finally gives me back my poem on the West Island with a B- written in the top left margin. Next to it, she scribbled her only comment: "Use of crude substantives to avoid from now on". I'm so glad. The midterm essay I just turned over is chock-full of crude substantives.

This time, I stay in class for the whole period. Leaving now would be pointless anyway: at two o'clock, I have an appointment with my Rationality professor. Yes, I finally decided to take the plunge and asked for a meeting in his office. I wanted to see him mainly because of that kind little altruistic speech he gave us the other day, but also because of that blood-curdling episode at the student placement center. I told myself maybe he could help me in some way, making sense of that no-future degree I'm working so hard at getting. I want him to tell me how to find a job I'll love, how to thrive on the market. I know, he's not a career adviser, he's a Rationality professor, he's not even in the Literature department, but the Poet and the Playwright from my other classes intimidate me. The teacher from my fourth class, I don't even know what he looks like; I've never been in attendance, I just hand in papers through a girl I know. For Mister Rationality, I'm thinking: he's a professor, I'm sure he knows something worthwhile. Or maybe he can give me some references, I'm sure. It took me a while to work up the nerve to ask to meet him. I still felt sore about his "C-/I-know-you-can-do-better" billet-doux. But, having nothing to lose, the week before last, I went to see him and asked for an appointment. He seemed surprised but happy.

Our appointment starts on the wrong foot: aside from the fact that he's profoundly late because he's stopped on the way over to gossip with a secretary who should exercise caution whenever she plucks her eyebrows, he spends the first ten minutes talking to me about my school bag. How this kind of school bag is good for my back because I can strap it on both shoulders instead of wearing it slung over like his daughter who just started university here this year, yes, here, but not in this department, no, because she prefers to pursue other interests as she's studying in Visual Arts, so…

Very interesting. Still, maybe I should've kept my mouth shut and let him babble on, because as soon as I uttered an innocent "Speaking of studying…", I opened the door to a long, painful introduction. Totally unpredictable. He leaps in:

"So you're in Literature, right?"

"Yes, sir."

"Do you like it?"

"Yes, well… I like to read."

"No, I meant do you like that particular field of studies."

I fidget on my chair a little. I'm scared I'll say too much – so I say less.

"Literature's all right."

"Good. It's a field of studies I find extremely important, even essential. Literature should be included in every university program, any program. It's a good way to broaden one's horizons."

I silently watch him talk to me. He's sitting there, his glasses pinching the bridge of his nose, a still-steaming cup of coffee forgotten on a filing cabinet nearby, while he elaborates and extrapolates, his tone steady, his aim suddenly straight and devoid of any roundabouts. It's weird: even though he's sitting over there calmly behind his desk, I can feel him prowling around me. Even if he talks to me with his hands placidly folded under his chin, forming a confident shell, it's weird, but I can feel him spinning a web around me, like a studious spider. What's even weirder, is that today, I notice for the first time that he talks through his nose. I wonder if he's always been talking through his nose and I never noticed it before, or if he only talks through his nose now because he has a cold or something, or because his glasses are too tight.

Then, out of left field, he says, nicely:

"…that's why it's so hard to make it. Of course, you know who André Gide refused to publish when he was working for Gallimard?"

In my mind, the question rolls and coils on itself: I don't know what he's talking about. In the space of just a few seconds, the relaxed yet conscientious air that lingered in the deep of his eyes morphs into a surprised shot of contempt when he realizes I don't know the answer. Because my paranoia suddenly jumps up the scales, I feel like the question is not a question but a trap disguised as a question. That's when it comes to me with total certainty:

I've stepped onto a minefield. My Rationality professor is a Literature fanatic. Who would've thought?

Timid and self-conscious, I smile a little too widely before answering his question:

"I'm afraid I don't know."

"You don't know? That's funny. The answer is Marcel Proust, who had to self-publish his masterpiece, *À la recherche du temps perdu*. I thought everybody knew that."

Marcel Proust? I see. Deep down, I really couldn't care less but I smile again, looking interested to be polite. The professor strikes again:

"But then surely you must know which bestseller cemented the reputation of the Éditions Grasset?"

Once again, the question butterflies everywhere in my mind with no hope of safe-landing. I can't answer; I can't answer with an excuse, with a joke, with a dodge, with a change of subject. Nothing.

"No sir, I'm sorry, I don't know."

"*Maria Chapdelaine*, of course!"

My eyes suddenly light up, innocent.

"Ah, yes, I think I saw a TV movie about that once..."

It's only when I notice the professor burying himself in his chair, his face now a mask of complete befuddlement, that I realize I've made a mistake. I can see him struggling to look normal, less scandalized, in an effort to spare me. He doesn't say anything anymore. Me neither. We look at each other silently, he still perplexed and I still scared, for much too long. I eventually hang my head and play with a little piece of thread sticking out of my school bag. I hear the professor get up. His squeaky loafers carry him round the desk. He comes and stands next to me, sighing loudly through his tight nostrils.

I don't want to look at him, and instead still tug on the thread. From the corner of my eye, I can see him fold his arms across his chest.

"How long have you been a Literature student?"

"I'm graduating at the end of this term."

I can hear his eyes widen.

"This is your last session? And you studied here all this time?"

"Yes."

He leaves and sits down behind his desk again. Throwing himself back, he suddenly lets out a loud chuckle.

"That's a good one! Ha! Ha!"

For a moment there, I even wonder if I should laugh along with him. I'm not sure if he's laughing at my expense, or at my former teachers'. I stay put, frozen, while he chuckles again and sticks a hand in one of his drawers. From the magnanimous heights of his kindness, the professor hands me a bookmark with his name inscribed on it, from a very famous publishing house. His name, and his editor's, are written in golden letters.

"Here. You'll find the address of my publisher on the back. If you want to fill in the blanks, I mean culturally, you can start with that..."

Turns out my Rationality teacher is a published author... Who knew? I'm beginning to see where my C- came from. Sitting ever closer to the edge of my seat, I'm ready now to say thank you and sprint out of his office – but no, he's not done yet. He bombards me with more questions, just for the fun of it. No, sir, I don't know who

Jacques Brault is, no, I don't know if Marie-Claire Blais hides herself with her hair when she's being interviewed, no I've never read the literary magazine *Trop*, or any other literary magazine for that matter, no, I don't know who Mister NRF Collection is, no, I haven't finished *Notre-Dame de Paris*, no I haven't read the entire works of Anne Hébert, no, I wasn't thrilled by the *Refus Global*.

Fifteen minutes later, I'm on the verge of tears, throat twisted and constricted, thoughts all blurry, clouded by the shame I feel at knowing I don't know anything. I've had enough. When the professor stops to catch his breath between two volleys, I get up:

"Thank you so much for your time, sir."

He also gets up, still enthusiastic: he's so happy, convinced he's been helpful:

"Ah, glad I could be of assistance. See you in class, then!"

Right. I shake his hand and leave.

It's true, maybe I should've studied something else. I know I'm not cultured. My interests are simplistic, common. I'm part of the people, the masses. I like reading biographies and watching action movies, tending flowers and tilling the garden, riding my bicycle and going for a dip, having a beer with Nicky and mowing my mom's West Island lawn. I went through the entire "Popular Culture" section at the municipal library – because that's me: I have a popular culture. I know I don't know anything of importance, but everything's valid. Knowing Zola wrote his novels in three days or three months is of no real importance. To each his own.

When I get on the subway, on the way back home, I throw my professor's gold-plated bookmark right into the first available garbage can.

# 20

The GT's tonight. If all goes well, the GT starts in two hours, assuming Guss will call. Nicky's still adamant: she's not coming. I hate getting ready alone, anticipating the worst. Having too much time with myself before a party is not a good thing. It's the perfect setting for worrying about all those "what ifs": what if Larry comes, what if he doesn't, what if Guss makes a fuss again, what if Miguel's angry at me for giving him the heave-ho, what if Gamache throws up beer on me like last time – what if, what if, what if.

For the past three hours, I've been torturing myself in front of the mirror. I've been trying on some clothes: too big, too small, too loose, too old, nothing fits. So far, I've shoehorned myself in and out of two dresses, and tried on and discarded three skirts and four pairs of pants, all of which were the height of underground fashion, three years ago. I've also tried to do my hair: everything crumbles, all the hairstyles literally melt around my face. I really hate being alone for this, it's mortal. And I mean, what's the point anyway? If Larry opts out, the whole evening's ruined as far as I'm concerned. And if he actually does shows up, it's almost as bad; I know I'll spend the entire time giving him the eye and pretending not to. God, I don't feel like going anymore.

I look at myself in the mirror again. I've had a couple of dizzy spells in the last few minutes, with little black spots dancing in front of my eyes. Nerves again. For a moment there, I wonder if I shouldn't gulp down a pre-emptive beer or a few downers, just to relax, to get loose faster.  But no – I'm driving tonight, so no messy intakes.

Instead of repeating the errors of my ways (changing clothes again and trying to curl, straighten, gel or pony-tail hair that's presently at its best under a shower cap), I try doing my makeup.  A little mascara, just a touch.  If I put on too much, the thing turns into goo and makes me look like a raccoon.  Oops, I just dropped the tiny mascara brush. God, my hands are actually shaking.  What was I thinking?  I should just do what Nicky said I should do, and forget the whole thing.  Follow her advice.  Follow my instincts.  And not go, not go, not go.

The phone rings while the mascara runs and I struggle to beat my hair into submission.

"Hello?"

"Hey Laurie, it's Guss."

"Oh hi."

A little nervous spasm makes me blink.  Alarmed, I look at myself in the mirror: I've just stamped my lower eyelids with two big black mascara blobs. Okay, okay, I'll fix that later.

On the phone, Guss is laughing, I don't know why. Meanwhile behind him I can hear a cacophony of voices laughing also, and talking in run-on sentences, joyously. Guss speaks up:

"So, are you coming or what?  'Party's already started."

"Where are you now?"

"I'm at Yohan's.  That's where the GT's at."

"Yohan?"

That's a surprise. Yohan's not exactly a party-giving kind of guy. He's definitely more a parasite than a host. Guss insists:

"So? 'You coming?"

Remembering Nicky's words of wisdom, I evaluate the situation at a distance, so as to not compromise myself by answering too fast:

"Who's there exactl…?"

Before I can reach the end of that question, I suddenly hear Larry's voice humming nonchalantly, whistling and singing an old pop song. Guss answers over the tune:

"There's Yohan, Steve, Gamache, Cyn and Larry…"

Larry's song suddenly stills. I can hear him ask "Who's on the phone?" to Guss who answers "Laurie". Guss speaks into the receiver again:

"Just a minute, Laurie. Larry wants to talk to you."

While Larry gets on the line, I look at myself in the mirror: with my pasty mascara and drooping hair, I'm the picture of misery. Fantastic.

"Hi Laurie!"

"Hey. How are you?"

Instead of answering, Larry starts humming the same song again.

"That's lovely, Larry. I'm impressed."

My tone's a little dry, a little sarcastic, but that's just because I'm feeling uncomfortable and have no intelligent reply at the ready. Larry stops singing.

"Are you coming?"

"I guess."

"All right. See you later."

"Right."

"Hey Laurie?"

"What?"

"Don't forget those pigtails!  Bye!"

He hangs up.  After a moment's hesitation, I decide to hop in the shower again: I *have* to wash out those big droopy curls and get rid of the mascara blob-thing. Pigtails won't do either.  I can't focus, God, I feel ill.  My stomach's all bundled and bungled.  A real urge to vomit suddenly takes me over the sink, post-shower, while I'm brushing my teeth.  I know if I think about it too much, I'll spew all over the place, for sure.  So without further ado I whisk myself away, I sprint out of the house wearing a casual pullover/jeans combination under my coat.  Sans makeup, sans pigtails – au naturel.  Determined, I throw myself in the car and drive down to Yohan's at full speed, trying to shake off the panic-vomit that still tails me on every twisted corner, at every walloping stop.  I'm nauseous the whole way over, even when I get out of the car, even as I move towards the apartment building and up the steps, ring the bell and see Guss open the door.

"You didn't bring any beer?"

That's the first thing he says to me while I get in and take my coat off, in silence, intently listening to my stomach.

"What's the point of showing up without booze?"

"I guess I'll just have to drink yours, Guss."

He laughs and shows me into the living room. Yohan's apartment is modest, but pleasantly so.  It used to belong to his mother.  The furniture's frugal, especially here in the living room, which acts as a cornerstone to the whole place.  Opening straight from the front door, the small expanse swells, then immediately resorbs into a narrow passage leading to the kitchen, on the left. On the far left, another anorexic corridor leads to the bathroom and, further down, to two small bedrooms. Everything is off-white except for the deep brown short-haired carpet that runs everywhere. There's no light switch. A single bare lightbulb hangs from the ceiling, with a little chain to turn it on or off.

Everybody's here already. Miguel added himself to the group in the time it took me to drive over. He's even grumpier now, at close range, than shafted over a phone. I think I've never seen him this discontented but I don't care. I sit between him and Cyn, on the only couch available, a yellowish white sectional mess of rags and sags.

Cyn's in top form tonight. She's wearing a see-through blouse that reveals her cleavage whenever she bends down. Her cherry-red hair hangs in long, straight strands. It shimmers in warm hues under the glare of the lightbulb. Cyn loves men and men love her right back. She gives herself to them instantly, wholly, and that's part of her charm. Nothing in her is cheap or complicated. Presently she takes me in her arms and kisses me, offering me a little smile, like dispatched from afar. I immediately catch on: she dunked her mind in something illicit before coming over – she's stoned solid.

Strange to say, my stomach flattened and placated itself since I've spotted Larry; I'm no longer nauseous. I can see him now, in the kitchen with Gamache; he smiled when he saw me come in. I'd like to look at him some more, but I'm pulled away from him by Yohan, who squats in front of me. The words in his mouth clink together:

"Well, Laurie. Glad you're here. I didn't think you'd come. Maude decided not to when she found out Nicky wasn't. Too bad for her."

No Maude? I see. I look at Yohan again, more closely. He's even more remote than Cyn. I think he can't even really see me. Cyn whispers in my ear "He's on pepe". I get it: Yohan and peyote have a long-time, deep-rooted association. Yohan's the kind of guy who took mescaline when he was ten, stole cars at twelve and had been arrested six times by the time he was fourteen.

I take him by the shoulders and kiss him on both cheeks, happy to peer into his diffusely happy smile. Yohan beams back at me, a little dazedly, then he gets up and leaves, but comes right back with a beer for me. How nice. He leaves again, this time to hook up with Larry and Gamache, still wheeling and dealing in the kitchen. As a sideline, Cyn starts cutting hash with Guss and Steve. This leaves only two entities without an occupation: Miguel and his constipated air.

As for me, my entire thought process is absorbed by that "Hello" I'm planning for Larry. Maybe he'll kiss me off to the sides, like I just did Yohan. Maybe he'll take me in his arms again and I'll be able, if only for a moment, to press my face against his neck and take in the deep warmth of is body... I can't help it, instead of waiting around and feigning indifference, I get up and head straight for the kitchen, heeding the call of Larry's distinctive laughter – but the doorbell rings. Yohan sticks his head out of the kitchen and, seeing me there, he cries out:

"Hey Laurie, answer that, will you?"

I double back bad-temperedly to the front door. There, a surprise awaits me: the newcomer is Peter, the clean-cut guy from the beer bash. He stands there, like struck dumb for a moment. Then he smiles.

"Oh it's you! Hi. How are you?"

"I'm fine."

I move aside to let him in. He points to himself, still smiling:

"You don't remember me. We met at the bash…"

"Yes, I remember you. How are you, Peter?"

"I'm all right. Your name is…"

"Laurie."

"Laurie, right, okay."

With that, he walks in and says "Hi, hi!" to everybody while everybody says "Peetee!!!" It's funny, he looks less straitlaced here than he did back at the bash. There's potent stubble on his face and he's wearing a dilapidated sweater; definitely a better fit. While I close the door behind him, he heads straight for the kitchen. I decide to forfeit my plan of talking to Larry, for now, and backtrack to my seat, between Cyn and Miguel. Having just finished a round of ht's with Guss and Steve, Cyn leans sleepily on my shoulder while I take a swig of beer. Miguel soon gets up, heaving an exasperated sigh. He goes to the bathroom, slamming the door behind him like he's trying to raise the dead. Cyn looks up, frowning, then turns to me:

"What's his problem?"

"Miguel? I think he's pissed off at me."

"At you? How come?"

I steal a glance at Guss and Steve. They're busy with their back and forth dope-taking; they don't care about anything else.  I hesitate again, wondering if I should or not, before finally opting to confide in Cyn and her vaguely intrigued stare:

"Just between us: Miguel asked me out a couple of weeks ago."

"What?  Miguel?"

"Yes, but shush!  I turned him down and I think he's still pissed."

"That's stupid of him, getting himself all riled up for that!  And you're not interested?"

"In Miguel?  No.  What's more, he's Sharon's ex."

"Oh, that's right.  She wouldn't like that."

Like a dutiful waiter, Yohan brings us a tray; on it are lemon slices, a salt shaker and a full bottle of tequila. Watching him leave and head back to the kitchen again, I must say I'm impressed: Yohan's deploying unsuspected qualities as a host.  Cyn looks at me kindly:

"Are you interested in anybody else, Laurie?"

I can hear Larry laughing in the kitchen again, goofing off with the other guys.

"Yeah, but I think I should forget about it…"

"Why?"

"Because I know the guy's not interested."

"Come on.  You *always* think that."

"So?  I'm usually right!"

Cyn smiles sadly.  Just then, Miguel bolts out of the bathroom like a rabbit on a highway.  He puts his coat on without saying a word to anybody.  Guss calls out to him:

· "Hey, Miguel!  Where are you going?"

"Liquor store."

With that, he slams the front door behind him. Cyn knits her brow:

"That guy's too intense."

We sit in silence for a few minutes. Casting aside my beer bottle, I tow in the little table Yohan set the tray on, with the lemon, the salt and the tequila. Cyn looks at me, concentrating:

"What were we saying? Ah, yes! Who's the guy you're hot for?"

"I'm not hot for him. I'm just... interested, that's all."

A moment later, Larry coincidentally steps out of the kitchen, grinning widely. He walks over to us and takes Miguel's vacant seat next to me. While he looks on, I lick the side of my hand to down a shooter. Almost by accident, almost involuntarily, I drop a glance in his direction, a side-look with a wickedly coquettish smile. I don't know where that came from. This audacity, unusual in my case, surprises Larry but he lets himself get lassoed in. Inching closer, he closes the space between us. Looking at the scene from her vantage point, Cyn suddenly leans in and whispers in my ear:

"Oh... I know who your guy is..."

Thank God, her voice was low. Larry's demeanor hasn't changed: he didn't hear the comment. As I grab the salt shaker, Cyn gets up. She turns to me abruptly:

"I'm going to the bathroom now. But when I get back, I'm gonna tell him."

She laughs, dismissing my desperate silent pleas, and slowly walks the length of the little corridor that leads to the bathroom. Over her shoulder, she adds:

"Yes, you'll see, Laurie. I'll make it happen."

"Cyn!"

She shuts the bathroom door. Larry's still looking at me, his gaze clouded over. Stuck there and with no solution in sight, I proceed with my tequila shot. Larry watches me salt my hand:

"What's she talking about?"

"Nothing important."

I lick the salt and gulp down a shot. Larry hands me a lemon slice into which I bite with expert gusto. I can already feel the tequila burning its way into my stomach, but that's the least of my worries: taking my hand in his, Larry licks off some excess salt and then also throws back a shot of tequila. No lemon. Eyes half-closed, he smiles at me.

"If I may ask, Larry: what are you on, exactly?"

"What?"

"Your eyes are really hazy. What did you take?"

"Oh, nothing. I just dropped some acid."

For Larry, dropping acid is nothing. That's because he's been semi-continuously taking acid for the past five years now. Me, I can't stand hallucinations. I took PCP once and had "visions" for twelve hours straight; the bed I was on was breathing and people around me looked like cartoons. Never again.

Larry smiles but then he turns around.

"Would you massage my back for me, Laurie? Before I start tripping."

"You want a backrub now?"

"Yeah, before I start tripping."

Slowly setting down my empty shot glass on the table, I start rubbing Larry's neck and shoulders, soon extracting from him a series of embarrassing moans and groans.  Gamache sticks his head out of the kitchen to see what's going on.  He laughs when he spots us, although we're still properly seated on the sofa.  Peter also peeks into the living room, looking at me with an amused air.  For the first time since he got here, I notice that his hippie girlfriend's absent.  I think "Good" while the rest of that sentiment seeps into the deep of my mind.  I keep on massaging Larry.  Knowing how to give a good rub-down is one of God's gifts to me; it's just one of those inexplicable innate skills.  Larry's head languidly rolls backwards.

"Shit you're good.  Where did you learn to do that?"

"Nowhere."

"You're really good."

Cyn comes out of the bathroom.  Seeing me hard at work, she winks and says:

"So you told him?"

She spoke loud enough for everyone to hear. Without turning around, Larry asks:

"Told me what?"

I answer on a sober reflex:

"You owe me a beer for the one you half-stole from me at the bash."

Cyn looks perplexed for a moment.  Larry, who can't see her from where he's sitting, pretends to be insulted:

"What do you mean "half-stole"?  I barely took a sip…"

Guss chimes in:

"Larry's always screwing people over with their stash."

"Hey man, get bent."

Massage over.  Larry gets up to face Guss, who came over to get a shot of tequila.

"You always think everybody's ripping you off, Guss.  Remember that time you thought Gamache sold you parsley instead of pot?"

Hearing his name, Gamache steps out of the kitchen, followed by Yohan and Peter.  Gamache immediately harpoons Guss:

"That's right, you jackass.  You thought I did it on purpose."

"You *did* do it on purpose!"

"No way, man.  It wasn't me, it was Maude.  She's always taking our stuff."

"That's not true!"

"You bet your ass it's true!"

"Shut up!"

"You shut up!!"

Cyn snaps:

"Why don't you *all* shut the hell up?!"

The front door suddenly opens on Miguel, back from the liquor store with more beer.

"Will you guys stop shouting?  We can hear you from outside."

Gamache, Yohan and Larry all fold back to the kitchen, Steve starts bt-ing again with Cyn, Miguel takes off his coat, Guss smells the lemons with a suspicious air, and Peter sits next to me. He takes the salt shaker with his ring-wearing hand, licks his other hand and salts it. He does this for about half a minute, spreading salt all over, covering a lot of area.  Guss and I look at him incredulously.  I frown:

"I think you're good to go, Peter. You'll overdose on salt."

Peter laughs wholeheartedly, still salting.

"Death by salt. That's funny!"

"It's not funny, it's true. Salt also increases your chances of developing cellulite."

I'm starting to say stupid things. That's the beer/tequila mix talking. Peter still thinks it's funny. He grins:

"I don't have any cellulite."

"No? Lucky you."

"Oh, come on… You don't have any cellulite either, I'm sure."

"Are you kidding? I'm full of cellulite, full!"

Halting his salting, Peter looks at me hard:

"Okay… Where's all that cellulite of yours?"

His gaze, suddenly heavy with innuendoes, puts Guss ill at ease and he scampers off, joining Cyn and Steve in bt heaven instead. Meanwhile, Peter stays on target: he's waiting for me to *show* him where my cellulite lies. I look down at my legs. I slowly stroke the upper part of my right thigh, right up to my right buttock. Peter follows my hand, his salt shaker now suspended in midair. My voice is a little slurred when I answer him.

"I have some here."

"Really?"

His voice shadows mine, pacing in slow tones.

"Hmm… I'm not sure I believe that, Laurie."

I can't help myself: looking up, I plunge into his eyes. Eyes that peer into me undeviatingly, clear and open, acute and precise. While we look at each other, I'm surprised to find I prefer Peter's explicit stare to Larry's vacant gape on acid.  Blinking away, I grab my empty tequila shoot glass and fill it up again, but it's more out of the need to do something, anything, than from a real desire to drink.  Handing me the salt shaker, Peter leaves to get himself another glass from the kitchen.  On second thought, I shove the tequila aside and instead head for the bathroom.

## 21

Business done, toilet flushed, hands washed – I step out of the bathroom just in time to hear a loud clamour ringing out of the living room:

"We're not in freakin' preschool anymore!"

That's Guss.  He grouches, under provocation, while everyone else laughs at his expense:

"Look at that Guss, getting all excited…"

That's Yohan, in full sarcastic mode.  I stumble into the corridor, manoeuvering as best I can; I've been sabotaged by alcohol, it saps my fluidity, making all movements uncertain, pasty.  When I manage to reach the sofa, I'm surprised to find Sharon sitting next to Miguel. She got here while I was away.  She howls a joyful "Hi there!" when she sees me.  Meanwhile on the other side of the room, Guss is cowering in a corner, the victim of the others' mockery; most of them are sitting on the floor, in a circle, looking at him.  I sit down too, intrigued:

"What's going on?"

Gamache motions in Guss' direction, making him mope with renewed vigour:

"Guss' shitting himself because he thinks we're trying to force him to play spin the bottle."

I snap back to reality.  In the center of our circle, Steve's bt bottle has pride of place, standing there empty but enthroned as we all look on, subdued by its very existence.  I get it now: spin the bottle.  The last time I played was eons ago; I was with Cyn and three zit-faced nitwits, each of whom I had to kiss before ending the evening with the skinniest but prettiest of the three. Simpler times.

Everyone's still eyeing Guss, who's still shrinking in his own pants, his indignant air mollifying every time he looks at me. I know why he hesitates: if I play, he plays.

This calls for a quick assessment of the situation. Sitting with me, starting from my left, are Gamache, an all-smiling Yohan, Steve, Larry, Peter and Cyn. Miguel and Sharon are still on the sofa: Sharon looks at us, giggling, while Miguel wears the same sour face he had on before and after his trip to the liquor store. According to my calculations, there's three categories to choose from:

a) <u>First category, total yuckiness</u>: Gamache scores top marks here, followed closely by Guss, just because he's puppy-loving in my direction. I can feel my stomach turning again.

b) <u>Second category, medium yuckiness</u>: Steve. Yohan too, but the dried-out foam he's got on the side of his mouth makes him slide dangerously close to the first category. I think Miguel also qualifies here. I'd like to kiss him but that tight-assed attitude he's got on is a major turn-off.

c) <u>Third category, improbable orgasm</u>: Larry. Of course.

I think it's safe to say: the stakes are anything but high. While I'm busy thinking, I feel sort of queasy – observed. Looking up, I see Peter there. He makes a funny little mien and subtly points to Guss, just to make me laugh. A brief smile of complicity passes between us. Peter. Right. I forgot to rank him. Clearing my throat, I try to recoup my composure, which in turn makes Peter laugh like we're in league with one another. I decide to play.

Steve and Larry now turn their attention to Sharon and Miguel, trying to convince them. Steve shows them the new joint he's just rolled:

"Hey, Sharon, if you play I'll let you smoke it all by yourself!"

Sharon yields and sits with us. She acts like the all-for-one joint appeal motivated her decision, but that's all pretence: the fact is that she's attracted to Steve (Cyn told me). I can't help but wonder why. Steve's a tall guy, well-made, with broad shoulders and good, solid hands. He could be handsome if it weren't for that face of his; his big head looks like it's been force-screwed unto his neck. He's also got this interminable mouth that circumnavigates his cranium. Aside from that, he's forgetfully ordinary: inaudible, invisible, unusable. Anyway.

With Sharon now sitting between Larry and Peter, our circle is nearing completion. In the midst of the clamoring still surrounding Guss and Miguel, Larry singles me out:

"Laurie! You're playing, right?"

No one except Guss pays attention to the question, or its answer. I nod at Larry.

"Yeah."

He says "Great!" looking satisfied and Guss, who was waiting to see what I'd say, now suddenly sits down between Gamache and me. He gets a round of applause from Yohan and Steve who both quickly pan around to concentrate their efforts on Miguel. Largely embarrassed, Miguel struggles to the last before finally forsaking his moral dignity. He sits down between Larry and Sharon. All positions have been filled. Gamache grabs the bottle excitedly, but I interrupt him:

"Hey, wait a minute! We don't even know what we're doing here, or exactly what?"

My sentences are a bit muddled. Gamache frowns at me. With his gargantuan body and baritone voice, he could be majestic and solemn instead of gross and vulgar. He leans towards me menacingly:

"What? What was that you said?"

Larry answers for me:

"She means: we don't know yet what we're spinning the bottle for."

I add:

"…and what we do when we land on a same-sex person."

Yohan lies recumbent:

"Shit, that girl's organized!"

Everyone laughs. Gamache nods.

"Okay, you're right. Let's see: when you girls land on another girl, you kiss her. If a guy lands on a guy, they pass."

Predictable outcry from us girls. Cyn, Sharon and I verbally rise in protest:

"Hey!"

"That's not fair!"

"If *we* kiss, then *you* kiss!"

Big chorus of disapproval from the guys. Gamache instantly rebels against me:

"Are you out of your fucking mind?  I'm not touching any guy with a ten-foot pole."

I shrug:

"Too bad, then.  Anyway, you don't have to neck or anything.  Just a peck and that's it."

"Forget it."

"All right.  No deal."

Everybody protests, interrupting and talking over everybody else.  Guss' right; this is preschool-level stuff.  Yohan has a sudden, rare lapse of lucidity.

"Yeah but hold on a minute: there's only three girls here, and…"

He starts to count but grinds to a stop halfway:

"…there's a lot more guys."

Larry expands on the thought:

"That's true.  We'll have to compensate."

I think things over before restarting negotiations with Gamache:

"Right.  We'll compensate.  Two in three: if you land on a guy, you pass and spin again.  If you land on a guy again, you spin again.  But the third time you get a guy, then you have to kiss."

Guss gets up in protest:

"I'm not playing!  All that kissing guys stuff is disgusting."

Meanwhile, Gamache sizes me up, deep in concentration.  Everyone looks on in silence, waiting for his verdict while Guss sways uncomfortably on his feet.  Yohan leans into Gamache's ear and whispers loudly like we can't hear him:

"Say yes!  Landing on a guy three times in a row is like one chance in a million!"

After another moment of tension, Gamache extends his hand to me:

"Right. You've got a deal."

We shake hands firmly. In pure agony, Guss reluctantly sits back down next to me. Feeling confident, Gamache spins the bottle first. My stomach gets all knotted up again, just thinking it could land on me. The bottle slows down and stops, pointing Peter. With his face a full mask of disgust, Gamache snatches back the bottle. Peter says dryly:

"Spin it again, man."

Gamache flicks the bottle with his big index finger. Everyone follows the thing as it twirls and finally peters out in front of Cyn. Gamache gets up, happy, while Cyn laughs nervously but with some genuine enthusiasm. I'm feeling nauseous by extension.

Gamache and Cyn kiss quickly and I shoot more tequila. Guss says to me:

"You're on a roll…"

We watch Cyn spin the bottle. It stops in front of Larry. I get a few pangs of envy, all involuntary, when I see his face light up and Cyn's features brighten in kin. She gets up and goes to him. Her way of walking, with that little foxy bounce she has, draws everybody's gaze. God, she *is* pretty. In a short moment, she's there already, leaning into Larry: as she does so, he drapes his hand behind her red hair, in a curiously tender gesture. I look away but stumble on Guss, who's offering me a bag of salt and vinegar chips. I decline:

"I don't think eating salt and vinegar chips before kissing someone's a good idea, Guss."

Guss stares down at the bag in puzzlement, then answers through a mouthful:

"Oh shit, I forgot!"

Larry spins the bottle. I can hear my heart palpitating every which way while we all look at the thing, spinning and spinning ceaselessly. It stops in front of Gamache. We laugh and Larry spins again, more forcefully. I try to relax. The bottle stops and points to Peter, who quickly hands it back to Larry. With an even more forceful flick of the wrist, Larry sends the bottle spinning, telling it "Come on, fuck, come on."

When the bottle lands again in front of Peter, everybody laughs and taunts the two guys, both of whom are now visibly shrinking at the thought of what awaits them. Meanwhile, a strange kind of lightning-bolt excitement runs through me. I watch as Larry gets up, chuckling to quell his nerves while Peter readies himself, telling us "Bah, it's just a kiss…" before saying to Larry "…but make it quick." I look at them getting closer, Larry putting his hand on Peter's shoulder while their faces flip on opposite sides. A blinding flash of sexual tension takes me over, melting all my resistances in an instant; Larry and Peter kiss, very briefly. Peter wipes his mouth with the back of his hand, making everyone roar. When he takes his turn spinning the bottle, I catch one of his glances branching off in my direction. Pretending I didn't see that, I down another shot of tequila, feeling it burn everywhere – when I suddenly get smacked on the shoulder. It's Guss, laughing at my expense:

"Your turn, Laurie!"

The bottle is there, spread out on a full horizontal, pointing me.

Peter gets up and comes over while I barely realize what's going on.  Larry exclaims:

"Ha!  It'll be Laurie's turn to spin next!"

Peter kneels in front of me, a furtive smile stealing across his lips while he gently cups my face with both his hands.  I can feel his ring on my cheek and his mouth delicately grazing mine.  Then it's all over, he's getting up again, walking away and sitting back down again.  Larry hands me the bottle:

"Make it count!"

I spin that god-awful bottle and of course it immediately lands on Cyn.  Right away, we're given a full round of intense wolf-whistles, woo-hoos and other insightful comments.  As I lean into her, Cyn smiles up at me.  I tell her "Sorry" before kissing her in front of all the guys who applaud us like there's no tomorrow.  Her face alight with laughter, Cyn curtsies teasingly and spins the bottle again.

## 22

After tequila shot number whatsit, I decide to pack it in. I don't want to drink or play anymore. Anyway, I've already kissed everybody at least once, except Sharon and Larry. Tequila made me adventurous: my first and second guy-categories fused with the third, and I even sneaked in a little tongue-action with Steve. That's it. I get up with the floor slightly oscillating under me. Guss and Yohan have left the game too. They now haggle with the others, trying to recuperate the empty bottle, which they want for themselves so they can do more bt's. When he sees me heading for the balcony, Larry calls out:

"You're leaving?"

"No. Just getting fresh air"

He gets up:

"Yeah, I think I'll do that too. I'm hallucinating too much."

He follows me and we step out on the balcony. The air outside is invigorating but I'm bothered by my heavy head and Larry's by now full-blown acid trip. Down on the street, I can see my car, waiting for me. I point it out to Larry:

"I'm too drunk to drive."

With a sigh, I realize I'd like to go home.

"You know, you're the only one I didn't get to kiss."

His comment takes me by surprise. I didn't think he had noticed, in his condition. This time, I play fair:

"I know."

"That sucks."

"Yeah."

A strange thick silence hangs over us. I look at my car again. I wonder what my chances of survival would be if I threw myself over the railing to get there faster. Like he's expanding on my thoughts, Larry suddenly bends over the railing, one leg dangling over the drop. Scared he's about to leap over because he thinks he can fly on acid, I grab him by the shoulder. Panic streaks clear across my voice:

"Larry?!?"

"Ah… Fucking hell, Laurie. You're always so intense about everything…"

His tone, drenched with impatience and exasperation, cuts me deeply. I let go of his shoulder as he turns towards me, bending even further over the railing. Shutting his eyes, he grins awkwardly, like contorted by effort. He's so far away from me, in another world where reality and fiction mix and unmix. I get nauseous again; that balcony won't stop swaying.

Cyn steps out to join us. She laughs at Larry's precarious position:

"You're so stupid. If you think I'm impressed…"

Larry laughs too and steps off his perch. When Cyn made her entrance, his whole non-verbal changed. The arch of his neck ceded, his tight shoulders loosened. It's as if Cyn's presence comforts him – whereas mine makes him uneasy.

I let myself slide down to the floor, resting my back against the patio door. Cyn sits next to me and lights a cigarette. Larry looks at her with a taunting smile:

"Hey Cyn. Laurie's the only girl I didn't get to kiss."

Cyn loudly exhales and licks her lips.  She giggles:

"*I* kissed her.  Three times.  And the third time, she slipped me the tongue."

Cyn always had the knack of exaggerating and teasing a guy at the same time.  Larry's now at full attention:

"Is that so?"

"Yeah.  You like that, right, seeing two girls tongue-kissing?"

Cyn dropped her question with a closed face, a detached expression – but the flirt's there, very tangible.  I feel in the way now, excluded by that clandestine glance they just exchanged.  I get up.  Larry and Cyn look on silently.  When I close the door behind me, I can hear them pick up their conversation.  Back inside the apartment, no one plays spin the bottle anymore, thank God.  The living room is now dotted with cliques: Sharon and Miguel are talking together, curled up on the sofa.  Steve, Yohan and Gamache are still smoking dope, and Guss is having a discussion with Peter.  That's where I head.  When he sees me coming, Guss automatically moves aside, making room for me next to him:

"So Laurie?  How d'you like the party so far?"

"I'm tired.  I'd like to go home, but I can't drive."

Guss throws himself at the opportunity:

"I can drive you!"

Gamache, who zeroes in on Guss' enthusiasm, even at a distance, firmly intervenes:

"No Guss, you can't drive her.  We need your car to get the rest of the dope from Yanni's."

Guss feebly protests:

"How come?  We've got more than enough here. I'll just go and drive her and come back."

"No.  We're leaving in five minutes.  Yanni's waiting for us. If we don't show up, he'll fuck off with the stash."

Standing like he does, with his arms folded across his chest tightly, Guss looks like he's about to deliver a good, categorical riposte – but he says nothing.  Peter settles his beer on the table:

"I can take you home, if it's not too far."

Guss answers in my place:

"It's far.  I better take her myself."

I let my guard down:

"It's a ten-minute drive from here…"

While Peter says "Fine", Guss pleads with me:

"Why don't you wait for us to come back from Yanni's?  I'll take you home then."

"Well, I don't know…  When are you coming back?"

"An hour, at the most."

And that's when it happens.  I see it as it unfolds, in real time: out on the balcony, Larry and Cyn are in a clinch, kissing each other passionately, almost falling backwards from the urgency of their embrace.  Searing pain instantly stabs me; my legs give way like they've been cloven in half but I remain strangely standing, transfixed and incapacitated.  No one noticed the incident and Guss is still smiling hopefully, waiting for my answer. I can't speak, I can't breathe.  I can see Cyn running her fingers through Larry's hair, her hand pressing the nape of his neck hard, Larry leaning into her, kissing her open-mouthed.  His eyes are closed.

In a blind dash for survival, I suddenly leap forward, startling Guss and Peter:

"Thanks Guss, but I have to go."

I sprint over to the front door, grabbing my coat on the flyby.  I'll walk home if I have to.

I've been walking for about five minutes. When I left Yohan's apartment, dazed and wounded, I thought I would perish before reaching the first street corner. I was wrong. In the cold air that lashes my face, as I slowly sober up and come to my senses, I realize that all that heartache for Larry's not really heartache. The point gets clearer and clearer, on every step I take, it's clear now that I don't feel that sad, not really, and that what I thought would be sadness is instead some sort of shame at a smear on my ego. I've wanted something I couldn't have because I couldn't have it. All this for Larry who's always stoned, has no drive, no common sense… and no interest in me. I almost laugh at myself: come on, I already went through the exact same thing, for the exact same guy, years ago. What would Nicky and J.F. think? Nicky would say "I told you", and J.F. would say "So what?" or "You'll get over it."

Walking at a brisk pace, I try J.F.'s tactic, "So what". Larry loves Cyn? So what. I'm walking home all by myself and it's dark and it's really cold? So what. I'm tired, it's late and the wind's cutting through my coat? So what. I'll never get Larry or any other guy ever again in all my life? So what. So what, so what.

What's funny is, over time, that little trick of J.F.'s actually works. I suddenly feel more at peace with myself, so much calmer in fact, that I'm beginning to wonder if I shouldn't just walk back to my car and drive home, carefully. But on the off chance I might see Larry and Cyn smooching on the balcony again, I change my mind. I'm still fragile. I'm better off walking anyway, it'll give me time to sort out my thoughts. Larry and Cyn, so what, Larry and Cyn, so what. It's working! I feel ounces lighter.

I'm busy sending mental waves of gratitude to J.F. when a passing car slows down next to me. It honks. The whole thing creeps me out, so I keep on going, not even looking up. The car honks again. This time, a voice also calls out to me:

"Laurie! It's me, Peter!"

I stop walking and turn. The headlights blind me for a moment, but I can still make out Peter's face, smiling at me, waving an arm that's jutting out of the window, beckoning me over.

"Oh, I didn't recognize you!"

"Get in!"

His voice is resolute, filled with undisguised relief at having found me. I smile and quickly climb aboard. Rolling up his window, Peter rubs his hands together, for warmth.

"Come on. I'll take you home. Where do you live?"

"That's nice, thanks. Go straight, then take the boulevard, and I'll tell you when to turn."

Peter puts the car in gear again and we're off. I feel reassured: honestly, I much prefer being here with him in his comfortable car than walking alone, out in the cold. It would've taken me at least an hour to get home. Peter glances over, amused.

"You left so fast! I didn't even get the chance to get my coat."

"I made up my mind of going on foot, that's all."

"It was that urgent?"

"It was."

He laughs with a shrug, then enquires:

"How long have you known Yohan, Gamache and Larry?"

Larry's name stings me. So what, so what.

"I guess I've known them for about five years."

"Funny how we've never really talked before, you and me."

"Yes, well, I haven't seen the guys in a while. We don't have that much in common anymore."

"Ah… You're in college now?"

"College?"

"Yeah, where the beer bash was…"

"Oh… No, I'm a university student. Almost done too."

"Oh. I'm still in college."

My thoughts drift slightly away from Larry. I ask:

"Aren't you older than us, though?"

"That depends. How old are you?"

"Twenty-three."

"Yep, I'm older. Twenty-five. I took time off after high school."

"I see. Turn left here."

"Okay."

"My house is on the third street, on your left, the second house, on your right."

"Third street on my left?"

And he turns on the second street. I giggle:

"No, no, not the second street! The third street, and the second house!"

"But that's the third street!"

"No, we're on the second street. We'll have to turn back."

"Doesn't it come around eventually?"

"It does, but it'll take longer."

We laugh together. A deep calmness washes over me. I feel really good. Peter winks at me as he puts the car in reverse and turns around to see where he's going. Even though he's careful, looking over his shoulder, he hits a plastic garbage can someone left out on the street.

"Shit."

Peter laughs at himself while he's putting the car right. Looking at him as he smiles self-deprecatingly, I get mischievous; to muddle the waters, I give him topsy-turvy directions, making him turn and detour through a complex weave of side-streets and one-ways. Aware of my littles scheme, Peter plays along:

"Didn't we just come through here?"

"No, no…"

"Are you sure? Yes, look, there's that signpost again."

"No. Different signpost."

We chuckle in unison, but soon I feel guilty about wasting his fuel just to fool around. I give him the right directions and we get back on track again. Peter heaves a reticent sigh:

"I'm starting to get the munchies…"

"Me too. I'm hungry… I ate a few chips back at Yohan's but that's all gone now."

"I haven't eaten anything since lunch."

I'm impressed:

"I can't hold out that long. Four hours is my maximum."

"Yeah? My brother's like that, too. He takes granola bars everywhere he goes."

I smile on that notion but soon my culinary musings veer off to include that huge St. Honoré cake my mom bought yesterday. It's still in the fridge. My mouth waters at the thought:

"Back home, there's leftover cake. There a good half left, I saw it before I went out."

"Your family will have eaten that by now."

"No. I live alone with my mother and she's off to work."

"Ah."

Peter concentrates on the road ahead. I look down at my knees. They were shaking from the cold when I got in the car. Now, nestled against the thick upholstery, enveloped by the hot air gushing out from the heater, my legs go limp, asunder. Swathed in volutes of warmth, my whole body feels iridescent. I wonder if that's the tequila again, in delayed-action. Something here is soothing; there's no stress, no malaise. No palpitating heart either, no quavering or anxious thoughts. I feel so good, I could almost fall asleep – but I can see my house, already looming in the distance. Two more intersections. With a heavy, drowsy voice, I phase out our silence:

"Would you like to have some cake?"

"What?"

"Cake. Would you like some?"

Peter looks hard at me:

"You wouldn't mind?"

"No… You're hungry, I'm hungry. You can come in if you want."

Peter looks at the road again. I watch him as he weighs his options. His little preoccupied air changes into a smile again:

"All right. I accept. If you're sure it's no bother."

"No bother at all. By the way, how much do you want, Peter, for the lift?"

"Oh, don't worry about gas money."

He hesitates, then his smile broadens again:

"You can pay me in cake."

I smile too, letting my head roll back languidly, watching his delicate fingers slide on the steering wheel. We glance at each other again, for a second – his gaze is fixed, decided; there's no doubt there. He stops the car in front of the house I'm pointing at. We're here. Peter turns the motor off and sits for a moment, staring ahead a little blankly, rubbing his chin. I can hear his stubble rasping against the skin of his hand. That soft sound, barely a murmur, unsettles me. I stay put, hesitating, with my hand shoved in my coat pocket. Inside, I can feel my house key, metallic, sharp. Peter turns to me. He doesn't say anything. I can't look at him anymore.

"Let's go."

I said that quickly, a little curtly even, to get rid of that awful lull between us. Peter nods:

"All right."

I open the car door. Peter does the same over on his side. The cold instantly coils around my ankles. Outside, gentle snow is falling in quiet detached flakes. The street is deserted and dark, with the windows in the houses around us unlit. Things seem stilled, motionless.

Peter lets me pass in front of him, gallantly supporting my elbow as I climb up the steps to the front

door.  I'm in a hurry to get inside, to get out of the cold
and shorten this in-between.  I feel pressed for time,
somehow, crushed by an inner emergency, a desire that
swells too fast, in vague proportions.  Stopping at the door,
I take out my key and stick it in the lock while Peter comes
up behind me.  His body, indistinctly outlined over my
shoulder, makes me febrile, impatient.  I give the key a
brutal turn and it yields.  The door opens wide.  I enter the
house and Peter steals in behind me, in one dash.  He shuts
the door, slamming it with a loud bang.  As I turn to face
him, he pins me against the wall, with the whole weight of
his body thrown upon me.  In one faultlessly-timed move,
we both lurch forward and kiss, crudely and full-on, with
no premises.  His hands rough at my coat, parting its folds
outright.  I hear the fabric tear.  Surprised, I breathe out of
turn.  Balance fails me.  While I pitch backwards, Peter
drives his legs between mine.  I can feel him there, ready.
I find my footing again and sink a hand in his pants.  As I
steadily mold him, Peter softens his grip on me.  Stroke
upon stroke, I bring him out, then let myself slide down by
degrees, face pressed against him.  Soon he's moaning
loud and long, arching his back, holding my head with
both hands.  I take my time pleasuring him, looking up at
him without stopping.  Moments later, gazing into my
eyes, he slowly pulls away and lays me on the floor, over
our scattered coats.  Pulling on my hair, tilting my head
back, he kisses me again and I answer him, matching his
deep, runaway stabs.  Somewhere in the fray, I hear a
condom being unwrapped as Peter sprawls over me, full
length, pushing one of my legs aside with his knee.  I
caress his face, breathless as he penetrates me.  Quickly,
our movements proceed from gentle to piston-like hard.

Grabbing my hands, he holds them over my head, clasping my wrists tightly.  Feeling cornered and wedged in, I start to come, right then and there, Peter brings me to full orgasm, provoking his own discharge by the same token. Our motion eases on a slow downshift, eventually grinding to a halt.  Peter rests his head in the hollow of my neck while we recuperate.  He takes me in his arms:

"Hold me."

I comply and hold him while he sighs, extenuated. He kisses me again while I enjoy the smell of his hair, which I never noticed before.  I smile when I see our clothes, still spread around us in a mingled heap:

"Hey, Peter.  Look at that."

He looks up and starts to laugh when he sees the mess we've made.  I slide from under him and start adjusting my clothes.  He looks at me for a few moments, raised on an elbow, then does the same.  While I'm busy hooking my bra, he gives me an inquisitive look:

"Are you all right?"

"Me?  Yes, why?"

"I just wanted to make sure you were all right and everything…"

I smile at him and we get up.  He puts his coat back on.  I extend a hand to shake his, business-like, but he reprimands me:

"Oh, no, not like that.  Come here."

He hugs me and kisses me on the cheeks.  I smile at him again:

"Well, goodbye Peter.  Thanks."

I correct myself:

"Thanks for the lift, I mean!"

"I know."

We laugh again as he steps out and I shut the door behind him.  I don't look out the window to see him get in his car, but I can hear the motor running and the car pulling out.  The sound fades in the distance.

I completely forgot about the cake.

24

"I can't believe it!  Larry and Cyn?  Oh, Laurie… The guy's shit.  I told you."

Nicky is very profoundly discouraged.  She smokes her cigarette, looking at me from her side of the table while we sit in the kitchen at my house.  She exhales:

"And screwing a guy you barely know!  Holy shit! What were you thinking?"

She's right.  What *was* I thinking?  Was I even thinking at all?  Did I have too much pent-up desire?  Was I too sex-starved?  Too drunk?  No.  I know I wasn't *that* drunk…

"Listen Nicky: the thing with Peter doesn't really matter, it doesn't count.  That kind of thing has no before, no after.  It's a one-shot deal.  It won't escalate into something à la Larry."

"I hope you're right."

Nicky stares at me, unconvinced.  I smile at her, convinced.

"I'm telling you, it's over and done with, so don't worry about it."

"Oh, I'm not worried.  But you, I know how you are…"

"Well I'm not worried either.  The thing with Larry is…  It pains me to say it, but I was stupid to think I still had a chance with him."

"So, what now?"

"What now?  Nothing now.  As usual."

Nicky pouts grimly.  I feel great.  Of course, when I think about what Larry and Cyn are probably doing at this time, hour, minute and very second, my feeling-great kind of dwindles a bit.

"Well, okay then, Nicky. I'm afraid that's it for today. I have to go to work, so…"

Nicky gets up, laughing again:

"So you're throwing me out?"

"Unfortunately I must, yes."

"All right. Say hi to J.F. for me."

"Will do. By the way, thanks for helping me get my car back from Yohan's."

"No problem."

I escort Nicky back to the front door. She suddenly stops dead in her tracks:

"You did it right *here*?"

She's pointing to the floor.

"I can't believe it."

She laughs, but then a playful gleam lights her eyes:

"On ten, how would you rate him?"

"Peter?"

"Yeah."

"Come on, Nicky. You know sex can't be rated. It's down to basic chemistry: either you click with someone and you have great sex, or you don't and you don't."

"Will you stop! How was he, on ten?"

I think for a moment while Nicky giggles. I reluctantly appraise Peter's artistry:

"Nine for timing. Nine for not wasting time on preliminaries. And nine for technique and execution."

"So all the way up to the nines? Well done, Peter!"

Nicky laughs again. Shaking her head, she exits, waving goodbye.

I'm supposed to leave for work in fifteen minutes. Fifteen minutes to take a shower, get dressed and pack my lunch. In the shower, I'm busy wondering if my stupid Community Center uniform is still in the laundry basket, when a surprise sensation hits me. It happens when I'm washing the nape of my neck: a flashback of Peter's hand grabbing me there emerges from the depths of my memory. It's been happening to me all day. Like a fragrance recalled, an afterthought of things recently past, I get flickers of last night's event that do nothing but revive that terrible craving I have for sex and more sex. The first time it happened was this morning, when I was eating my cereals. The smell of his hair, coming out of nowhere. Two hours later, it was the taste of his mouth, materializing again in all its delicious flavor. Then, again, right before Nicky got here, I remembered the sound of his voice, filtered through pleasure. It's terrible. It makes me want to do it all, all over again, and again after that. Good God. It's like a drug; the more I think about it, the more it consumes me. It's there, in my mind, when I dry myself, rubbing the towel between my legs, when I strap on my bra – even when I brush my teeth. God in heaven.

I'm late. I forgot to make myself a lunch and by the time I find something to bring over, I'm absolutely, perfectly late. J.F.'s already lounging in my glass tank. He opens his arms in a large demonstrative gesture when he sees me.

"Well, well now, ladies and gentlemen: for the first time ever, Laurie is late."

The "ladies and gentlemen" is purely for show: as always, we're alone in the office.  J.F. insists:

"And now I'm guessing you have a good excuse for this…"

I take my coat off and try to explain:

"I thought I had a lunch packed…"

J.F. points his index finger at me, in a pretence of menace:

"I'll let you off this time, but you better watch your step, young lady."

I sit at my desk:

"Did anything happen while I should've been here?"

J.F. leans nonchalantly against the doorframe:

"No.  The football Coach came back…"

"Oh no.  Did he lodge that complaint against me for the thing about the ice-rink?"

"No way.  He came in here, all happy, wondering where you were."

"Really?  Okay.  Anything else?"

"Yeah: Giles wants us to change the nets on the basketball hoops in the gym, if we can spare the time."

"Can we spare the time?"

"I doubt it."

While I shove my lunch bag under the desk, J.F. yawns and stretches.  He really looks upbeat today.  I ask:

"What's going on?  You look so happy!"

"I know!  I don't know why, but today I feel great! Like I've just had the fuck of a lifetime."

The words trigger me like a stimulus does a reflex: I sparkle from all angles in spite of myself.  J.F. immediately zooms in:

"No!!!  Don't tell me?!..."

Struggling, I make every effort to keep a straight face – but I can feel my cheeks burning.

"Oh my God, Laurie!!!"

"Stop right there!  Nothing happened…"

"Don't give me that!  You're bright beet-red!"

For one measly second, I dare to look up: completely beside himself, J.F.'s fidgeting all over the place from third-degree impatience:

"I was *right*!!!  You had sex!!!"

He throws himself in his wheelchair, overexcited:

"It finally happened!"

I laugh, embarrassed.

"Come on, Laurie!  Am I right?"

"Well… yes.  My God, it took you like two seconds!"

"I've found you out!  Ha!  Ha!  Sooooooo?  Was it sexy Larry?"

"No."

J.F. leaps out of his chair.

"No!?!  You mean it was someone else?!  Okay, now it's serious: I want details!"

J.F. sits back down again while I give him the short-medium version.  All the while he listens in absolute reverence, teetering on the edge of self-control.  When I'm done, he stays silent for a few moments, his face incredulous.

"And right there in the vestibule…  That's real passion!"

"I guess."

"Was it really torrid and everything?"

"I told you already."

"So you'll be going out with this guy Peter now, or what?"

"No, no. That was just a one-off…"

J.F. renews his smile.

"You have to admit, Laurie. Life is beautifully organized! Look: you were so discouraged by that thing with Larry, and then life steps in and gives you a good, nice hard fuck just to pep you up. That's so great…"

"Yeah, that's great…"

There's a hint of hesitation in my voice, which J.F. doesn't pick up. Soon he gets up again and goes downstairs to attend to some rare gym supervisor business. Once he's gone (whistling down the corridor, no less), I struggle with a weird memory mix of Larry and Cyn's ardent embrace and my own feverish intercourse with Peter. I get uneasy when a glimmer of hope, faint but growing, slowly floods my mind. What if what happened between Larry and Cyn was just as transient as what happened between Peter and me? What if all those fiery kisses of theirs led to nowhere? It's possible! After all, Cyn's not the kind of girl who gets hooked on a guy, she knows how to love and move on, she's a free spirit, she likes novelty… And Larry? Does *he* like novelty?

## 25

"And that concludes our journey through the many realms of Rationality.  Of course, I'm always at your disposal for last-minute consultations, if ever you should encounter difficulties in writing your end-of-term paper. As you know, I'm always ready to help out."

On these words, my Rationality professor turns to me for a long-held, self-satisfied wink.  For the past hour, I've given up taking notes, instead sighing in bundles every time he pontificates the other way.  Anything he says now just passes me by.

"So thank you for choosing this course.  I hope all of you will be brimming with ideas and inspiration to write that last paper!  Goodbye and good luck to you all."

While other students pack their things (I packed mine forty-five minutes ago), I grab my school bag from under my chair.  Leaning over, I spot my neighbor's watch and intercept the time.

"Sorry, but your watch says 5:05.  Is that right?  I mean, is that the actual time?"

"Yes, my watch's working fine.  It's precisely 5:05..."

The guy barely finishes his sentence.  I sprint out of the classroom, shoving people out of the way, pirouetting between obstacles, coat and schoolbag flailing all over the place, my bus/metro/train pass at the ready: if I miss the next subway, it'll be too late to catch the last train home.  Our class should've ended ten or even twenty minutes ago, but the professor kept on talking and talking and, somehow, I never noticed how late it was.  I run like my life depends on it. I've got to make that train, I've just got to make it! Luckily, I step onto the platform just as the subway pulls in. Ah… big relief. If all goes well, I'll slide on base for my metro/train connection, with a few minutes to spare, even. I'm so happy. Yes, even now, stuck here and standing in the midst of stifling strangers, out of breath and stewing in my coat, I feel happy. Even ever-growing hordes of people getting in at each station, pressing up against me and treading on my feet make me happy – as long as I catch that train. If I miss it, I'll have to make a complete U-turn, take the subway again, get out at Lionel-Groulx and wait in line to take the Lakeshore bus, which will slog through heavy traffic for another hour before dumping me in the backwoods of the West Island. No thanks.

Problems start about midway through my run: for some unknown reason, the subway stops and lingers for at least two minutes at EVERY station, doors ajar, motor hesitant. I'm beginning to get nervous. At that rate, I'll never make it, it takes too long, God, I'll miss the last train, I'll have to backtrack all the way downtown again, take the bus, get stuck in traffic on the highway, stand all the way and then walk twenty minutes to my car. COME ON!!! I'm tired, I'm hungry, it's too hot, I feel faint, I want to go home!!! The subway belches ahead again. Seeing it moving so slowly, I decide to take action: elbowing my way through the crowd, I reach the starting line, nose on the door, ready to dash out at Vendôme, the next station. I look at the time on the watch of the man standing next to me: my train comes in, in exactly fifty-four seconds (yes, trains are *that* precise). I know my energy levels are already down to naught. I'm not a sporty type, I've never been in top physical shape, but now I must do the impossible: sprint over a distance of a hundred thousand meters, hurdle over a first volley of stairs, then hop over a gate and flit through another flight of stairs and two heavy doors before finally hitting that train platform. The odds are definitely stacked against me but I'm ready: when the subway stops at Vendôme, the doors open – and I'm off!

Nothing can stop me. I don't even know who or what I'm stepping over or flinging aside: I don't care. Running wildly over things and people, I climb those flights of stairs four at a time, driven beyond all hesitation, motivated against all reason – and then, for a moment, I see it through the long glass window overhead: my train! Already pulling in. I can even hear its distinct, teasing little whistle, announcing its eminent departure! I crash through the last gate, running still. Only one flight of stairs left! I take it on, my stamina already waning, my heart pounding, with legs rebelling and lungs hurting as I struggle on, harassed and disoriented, completely outside myself; all those aerobics classes I registered in but never went to flash before my eyes. I must catch my train, I must catch my train, I must catch it – and then, I catch it. Or rather it catches me: right off the left temple. In my head, the shock cracks with a loud "bang!" reverberating in my cranium like the clinking spatter of sharp nails: I tried to get on the train while it was moving and it hit me. I didn't even *see* it moving. The train hit me head-on, on the head; I'm dragged by its momentum and thrown up in the air, landing with a thud on the platform, my legs less than a meter away from the wheels cutting across the rails. People rush over to help me while the train pulls away.

"Are you all right, miss?"

"Dear God, are you hurt?"

"You almost got yourself killed!"

I'm fine. I just have a huge bump on the head. A man with a large beard helps me up. My vision's a little off; everything's blurry. However I still smile at people to reassure them:

"Thank you, I'll be all right."

I can hear a collective sigh of relief. Somewhere in the back, next to the heavy gates, I vaguely notice a woman, looking at me with contempt: she thinks I'm utterly stupid. She's right. After one last polite smile, I walk off slowly, jelly-legged, to the far end of the platform. There, alone at last, I let myself fall apart. I weep for a long time, ashamed and remorseful. I weep right up until another train comes. Yes, as it turns out, the train that hit me wasn't even the last one after all. I'm so profoundly stupid. I'm also exceptionally lucky not to have received a concussion or had both legs sawed off. I don't know what or who protected me, if it was God or someone else, but I thank them by reciting five Hail Marys, one after the other, crossing myself devoutly each time.

Climbing aboard this train, feeling wobbly still, I can't hide my emotions: I cry again, this time in front of everybody, all the way back to the West Island. Crying in public is weird. There's this feeling of not having anything to lose anymore, of being invincible because, suddenly, all your insides are outside. One thing, though: deep down, I really wanted someone to come over and console me, and cuddle me, and tell me everything's gonna be all right, but people get embarrassed seeing someone cry, they look elsewhere, as if witnessing a stranger's distress is some sort of indecent act. Understandable; most of us don't know how to handle other people's pain, especially exposed pain.

I'm busy looking for more tissues in my bag when a hand lands on my shoulder. I look up with my red eyes: it's Ticket-Ticket. He's staring at me, visibly worried:

"What happened, sweetie?"

His gentle, soft tone finishes me off: I start crying all over again. All those tears I was almost able to bottle up come right back up to the surface. Having no strength left to control myself, I let go.

"The other train… I tried to get on it while it was running, and it hit me…"

While I tell the story, Ticket-Ticket shakes his head, incredulous.

"You know you should never try to get on a train that's moving… It's dangerous."

I start crying again, burying my face in my hands. I'm so ashamed.

"I think I'm okay… It's just that I was hungry, I was tired and I wanted to go home."

"Ahhh, yes, accidents always happen when we're tired or hungry or in a hurry. They happen so fast…"

I blow my nose and in a blink, I catch sight of a man sitting opposite me, on the other side of the aisle. He smiles at me compassionately. I try to smile back at him through my tears; his smile is so warm, so kind. Ticket-Ticket still has his hand on my shoulder. He leans into me, paternal:

"Where do you get off?"

"Beaconsfield."

"All right. Stay put, relax, and I'll come and get you when we're there. Meanwhile, try to take it easy."

I want to tell him "No thanks" because I'm quite sure I can still get a grip on myself, but he turns and leaves, taking fares from other commuters. I don't feel like calling out to him. Instead, I let my head roll back on the seat, feeling exhausted. God, I'd love to be back home already.

I must've fallen asleep because Ticket-Ticket wakes me up just as we're going through Pointe-Claire. The man who smiled at me earlier on is gone, his seat is empty. Ticket-Ticket helps me up and courteously escorts me to the door. When the train grinds to a stop, he even assists me in climbing down to the platform. As I gratefully accept his help, he gives me a little tap on the shoulder.

"See you soon and be careful now!"

"Yes. Thank you very much."

I smile at him hesitatingly, and he smiles back, hopping onboard again, brimming with selflessness and goodwill. The train slowly pulls out as I get into my car. I start the engine. While I wait for the motor to warm up, I rest my head on the steering wheel. Tears well up again, but these are not from pain, or shame or sadness; they're tears of thankfulness. I feel so grateful for having had, at that moment in my life, a man smiling at me warmly from his seat and a train controller who's so naturally generous and helpful, it's unheard of. It's times like these that make you think it's a good thing to be a human being and to have other human beings around. My mother once told me that the greatest love of all is not the passionate torrid love of lovers, or even the tender love of old spouses. No, she said, the greatest love of all is fraternal love, spontaneous love between two people who might not know each other that well, or even at all, but recognize they're one and the same, somehow.  When Mom told me that, I had no idea what she was talking about.

26

I sleep the rest of the evening, right through the night and the next morning, not even waking up when my alarm goes off. Needless to say, I barely grieve when I realize it's now 11:02 and I've just missed my second-to-last Dramatic Writing class. I get up in slow-motion and decide to take a shower. Wavering for a moment between putting on my corny shower cap or washing my hair, I finally climb in capless.

"Ouch!"

While shampooing, I happen upon that magnificent bump on the left side of my head, a souvenir from last night's runaway train. Like I could forget.

I take my time in the hot water. I heard my mother leave to go grocery shopping half an hour ago; I know she won't be back for another hour. So while I'm still by myself, I slip into some loose clothes and head for the study to take an envelope. When I got up this morning, I made a decision: today, I'm starting a new life. Maybe it's stupid, but my mind's made up: I'm taking action today. My near-train experience has made life that much more precious. I don't want to wait anymore, I don't want to wait for things to fall naturally into place. No, no more excuses. I'm taking the plunge, today.

I stick two pounds of stamps on the envelope, just to be sure, take out that letter from the drawer, run downstairs, put on my boots, grab my coat and my keys, quickly, quickly before I change my mind. It's today, definitely.

I'm halfway done shutting the door behind me in a great decisive flurry, when the phone rings. The answering thing's on, so I could just leave anyway, but I listen in, curious. I can hear my own voice: "Hi, leave a message, bye" and the sound of the beep. Guss' voice reverberates in the house:

"Hi there Laurie, it's Guss. I was just calling to see if you knew about Larry and Cyn. Did you know they're going out together now? I had no idea. Gamache just told me. Anyway, call me back, okay? Thanks."

I close the door. I try not to dwell on it, but it's no use; I dwell. So Larry and Cyn are going out together, they're dating, they're serious about each other, it's for real, it's forever. Shit. Driving along the boulevard, I realize I forgot to warm up the car. The dashboard blinks and the motor struggles and staggers while I try to ease up on the gas pedal. Larry and Cyn are going out. I try to concentrate on the road ahead, fifteen minutes on, plowing through mounting snow, driving right up to the letter box, buried in a big snowbank. I stop here and park right in front of a fire hydrant. I don't care. Larry and Cyn are going out. I must act fast now before I change my mind: I grab the letter and slip it into the overstamped envelope. As a return address, I write my own. As the addressee, I write my father's name, with his address underneath. Then I get out of the car.

Shoving the letter down the mailbox's throat, with snow up to my knees and snowflakes covering my face, I feel like a ton of bricks just lifted off me. For the first time since I don't know when, I inhale and exhale and feel well, both times.

I don't know when my father will get this letter I'm sending. I don't know what he'll think about those fifteen pages where I rant and pour my heart out, but I decided not to worry about that. I took action today, just to do something nice for myself, something new, to get rid of that rejected-girl image Dad left me with, and which Larry constantly reflects back to me. I did it to free myself of extreme boredom at work and unrestrained vacuity at school. I'm posting this letter for myself, to save myself, to give myself a chance. Just in case the next train doesn't pass me by.

When I get in my car again, I suddenly remember: there's a book I need to write my last Poetry assignment with. And Cyn's got it.

27

*The Metamorphosis* by Franz Kafka. Cyn borrowed my book just after the beer bash. She even came over to my house to get it before I left for work. At that time, my Poetry teacher had given no indication that Kafka was a potential candidate for end-of-term subjects. In her class plan, she had written "Thematic Study on a Poetically Inclined Author", which could include just about anybody. I mean, it was vague, and had I known this would happen, I would've kept Kafka in close proximity. I first read *The Metamorphosis* back in college, taking all those clever notes and writing them in the margins of the book. I need them now. It's important. My last Poetry essay just happens to be my very last university paper; excluding revisions, I'm done writing the others.

I decide to go through Guss, which is easy since he's usually so helpful and docile. Maybe he can even go get my book from Cyn's for me. What's more, I have the perfect excuse to call him because he left a message on my answering machine. Right? Right.

"Hi, Guss, it's Laurie. You called?"

Instantly, he's happy:

"Yeah! How are you?"

"I'm all right. You?"

"Great!"

"Good."

"Hey, did you know about Larry and Cyn?"

"…"

"I just found out!  Apparently, it's the real thing, too!  Apparently, they've been together every day, all the time, since the GT."

"Is that right?"

"Didn't you know?"

"No, Guss.  I had no idea."

Better play safe, just in case.  I might need to cloud that issue, later on.  You never know.

"Listen Guss, I'd like to know if you could help me out, here."

"If I can, I will!"

"I was wondering if you could get a book for me, from Cyn's.  I lent it to her but I need it back for an assignment."

"Oh…  I'd like to help you but I can't."

"Oh?  Why not?"

"Because Cyn's never even been home: she's still at Larry's.  She's been there ever since the GT.  Like I told you, they've been together ever since."

"I see.  It's serious?"

"Absolute passion, apparently.  Who would've thought, ha! ha!, that Cyn and Larry would end up together after knowing each other for so many years…"

"Yeah…"

"You know, Laurie, sometimes old friends make great couples…"

Guss' limpid allusion to our own friendship and his hopes of seeing it blossom into romance betrays something else in his voice, present since the start of our conversation.  I realize it now: he's actually *happy* to tell me about LarryandCyn.  Guss always suspected I had a weakness for his friend, and now it's his turn to gloat while

I founder, knowing my attraction for Larry is doomed. Irritation pulses through my voice:

"Guss, could you please go over to Larry's then, to get that book?"

"Why don't you go there yourself?"

There's so much malice inserted into Guss' tone, it's actually pitiful; all my feelings about how beautiful human beings are, and how we should all love one another, sink right back into oblivion.

"Listen Guss, my car doesn't work when it's snowing."

I know it's a lame excuse, but it's all I could come up with.

"Well, well, Laurie… You can call them yourself and find out if they can spare a minute from their love-fest to bring you back your little book."

He chuckles gently, like I can't hear him.

"Right, thanks, Guss. Bye."

I hang up, almost cracking the phone in the process.

On the off chance he's free, I call J.F. No answer. I can't believe he's actually unavailable to one of his callers, today of all days. I try Nicky. She answers.

"Hello?"

"Ah! Nicky? I'm so happy you're there! I need to ask you a favor."

"What is it?"

"I need *The Metamorphosis*."

"Kafka?"

"Yes! Do you have it?"

"No. Never read it. Is it any good?"

"Not bad. You don't have it, though, you're sure?"

"Yep, I'm sure. Why? You need it for school?"

"Yeah. I lent my copy, with all the useful tips and notes in the margins, to Cyn…"

Nicky hesitates for a moment:

"You don't want to ask her for it?"

I answer with a catch in my voice:

"Oh, Nicky… I can't. She's with Larry now, so…"

"It's serious?"

"Apparently."

Picking up on my sadness, Nicky answers compassionately:

"Okay. First, let's look at your options. Wait a second, I'll get my cigarettes."

"Okay…"

I hear Nicky set the phone down and walk around her little apartment. She comes back and exhales as she speaks:

"Okay, did you think about your first option?"

"Yes. My first option is not calling Larry and not getting my book back with all the useful notes in the margins."

"Uh-huh. Your second option could be calling Larry and getting your book back with all the useful notes in the margins so you can write that paper and finish your degree."

"Okay…"

"Then there's the third option: ask someone else to call Larry but not me because I have to be at a Parent-Teacher Seminar in twenty minutes. Which reminds me: Laurie, I'll have to hang up in five minutes to go to my Parent-Teacher Seminar."

"Duly noted."

"So option number four: you could get a copy from the municipal library instead."

"No, our library's too small. They just have popular novels there – I should know. No classics."

"Option five, then: getting a copy from the university library. That should take you, what, an hour on the roundtrip?"

"Three hours, you mean. And it snowed, remember? I'll have to pack a lunch. Also, it's the end of term: any and all important books will be long gone."

"Yeah, I guess you're right."

"Hey! Wait a minute, I've just had an idea: if you think about it, Larry and Cyn don't *really* know I'm attracted to Larry. I told Cyn about it at the GT but she was so out of it I'm sure she doesn't remember anything."

"There, you see…"

"Ah! Option number six: I could also ask Trifocals, the guy in my Poetry class…"

"Okay…"

"…but I don't know how to reach him and that would be, like, my last option because I think I'd rather call Larry than him, actually."

"And the way you've been talking about this guy, Trifocals or whatever, I'm sure he'll give you a sermon on "How to be better organized next time, in five easy steps"."

"That's true. Okay, okay! I've got it! Option number seven: I can try and write my essay from memory…"

"Oh, boy…"

"...okay.  Then there's option number eight: try everyone else I know to see if they have a copy."

"Come on, Laurie."

"I know, I know.  Makes no sense."

"Listen, you've handled other Larrys before.  You need that book to get your degree.  He's not worth getting *that* messed up about."

"No, you're right.  But still, it's humiliating. Maybe he'll think that the book's just an excuse to call him again."

"Nah, I don't think so.  And even if he does, who cares?"

Nicky starts laughing, and chanting, like she's part of a delirious crowd:

"Laurie!  Laurie!  Laurie!  Woo-hoo!  You can do it!"

"Okay, you're right.  It's my only option."

"It's your only option: you can do it!  But I have to leave now, my Seminar..."

"Oh!  Sorry about that.  Thanks, Nicky."

"No problem.  Talk to you later.  Bye."

"Bye."

We hang up.  I can do this.  I'm not tough, but I am strong.  I mean, I've been through worse things than this. Come on!  I am perfectly able to call him.  Right?  Right.

## 28

"Hello?"

"Hi, Larry?  It's Laurie.  Sorry to bother you…"

"Hey!  No bother!  I was watching TV and eating chips."

"In the morning?"

"It's almost noon, now."

"Oh, right."

"You're up late!  You're not in school today?"

"No.  I've slept through my alarm."

"Ha!  Ha!  I bet you were off partying last night!"

"Not really….  Err, I hear your life has taken a turn for the better."

"It has!"

"I'm happy for you, Larry, really."

"Yeah.  I'm happy too.  About time, don't you think?"

"I couldn't say."

"I was tired of being in that lonely hearts club, you know."

"The lonely hearts club?"

"You know what I mean."

"Oh, yes.  I'm the club President, actually."

"Ha, ha!  That's a good one!"

"Yes, well, anyway…  I'm happy for you and Cyn. I mean, you've known each other for a while…"

"I know, it's so cool!"

"Yes. Listen, Larry, I need to ask you a favor.  I'm calling because…"

"And I thought you were calling me so we could chitchat!"

"Well, yes, but I need a book from Cyn.  She borrowed it from me a couple of weeks ago.  When I spoke to Guss this morning, he told me she's at your place."

"What?  She's not here."

"She's not?  She's at her place, then?"

"I guess.  I haven't seen her in days."

"Really?"

"What?"

"Nothing.  It's just that… Guss said you two were *always* together."

"He's so full of shit.  I've seen Cyn only once since the GT.  We've been talking on the phone, mostly."

"I see.  Well, sorry to bother you.  I thought Cyn was there."

"Don't worry about it."

"Okay, I'll call her then.  Thanks anyway.  Bye."

"No problem.  Bye!"

Phew!!!  Thank you, dear God in heaven.

# 29

Cyn very kindly gave me my book back. She also gave me all the juicy, graphic details of her affair with Larry. Just as I thought: she had no recollection whatsoever of any interest on my part, or so I deduced. A good thing. It allowed me to take on a new role: the friend of the couple, the friend who's friends with both partners, in whom both partners confide when they want to talk about their partner. It's weird. But what's even weirder, is that part of me, minuscule at first but now expanding, actually started feeling genuinely happy for Larry and Cyn. Turns out Cyn had been Larry's dream-girl for the past three years, unbeknownst to any of us. And as luck would have it, Cyn had also pined for Larry for months on end, fighting against herself by having lots of sex with lots of other men when in reality all she wanted was to be in a serious relationship with him. So there.

I finally finished my Rationality essay on Michel Foucault and his criticism of modern society, I handed in my televisual play to my Dramatic Writing professor, and I chose to review *Candide* by Voltaire for my Early Modern Literature assignment. For my last university paper, the one on Kafka, I feel like writing something intelligent, but something that will remain intelligent and not become less intelligent over time or from wear-and-tear. I know it's a tall order, but I'd like to keep the teacher at bay, mentally, especially since she ruined my near-perfect grade average with that C she gave me for my midterm paper. She wrote on the cover page: "Again, too many crude words, Laurie. Did you read my comments on your previous poem?" – this, of course, without realizing she gave me back my poem *after* the deadline for the midterm paper. Whatever. Writing a supremely intelligent paper on Kafka is, I have to admit, a little beyond my skills: I know someone else will always be able to sweep away anything previously thought of as intelligent with something more intelligent. It's just a matter of time. And that someone could very well be my Poetry teacher, seeing as I'm sure she's more intelligent than how intelligent I think she is.

I'd just like to end things on a good note.

I've been completely luckless so far. I've tried writing my essay everywhere: at home, at the library, in the school cafeteria, even in the bathroom. As it stands, even those clever notes I had written in the margins are useless. Argh! I could vomit. I'm TIRED of writing for school. I have absolutely no inspiration, not one valid thought and no idea of where to begin, how to start. One last ultimate paper to write, one, and here I am stuck with writer's block. Oh yes. There it is. The blank page. How fun. After three years, a hundred and twenty essays, a hundred and twenty introductions, developments, conclusions, table of contents, annexes, supplements, bibliographies, all the footnotes, references, counterarguments, theses, antitheses, after reading more than five hundred reference books and five hundred more manuals to check those references, that's when, here, now, standing on the very edge of graduation, I don't know what to write anymore.

Back at the Community Center, J.F. looks a little dejected; he's mopping the main hallway like he's ready to drown himself in the bucket. His girlfriend, Eve, finally found him out after bullying him into admitting he'd cheated on her. Now it's all over between them. I'm pretending to read *The Metamorphosis* (yes, I brought my book, all my notes, two dictionaries and my anaemic first draft here at work), but I keep glancing over at J.F. While he still has his back to me, I observe his hunched shoulders, his stooping neck and trailing mop. It's a sad sight. I don't want to try and console him, though. That's the worst possible thing I could do. In that kind of situation, words just get in the way anyway. I remember one time when I was dumped by a boyfriend I really loved, I couldn't get over it, I was ill with pain for days: no food, no sleep, no hope of a life beyond that point. After a week, J.F. dropped by, just to see how I was holding up. He knew he couldn't say anything to make me feel better, so instead he took me in his arms, cradling me like a child, allowing me to cry freely. It's one of the nicest things anyone's ever done for me.

Poor J.F. It's terrible seeing him suffer like this, even though he says he just got what he deserved.

Kafka stares me right in the face, flattened atop my dcsk, one side slightly damaged, its cracked binding protruding haughtily. I still don't know what to write. J.F. enters my glass tank unceremoniously:

"I'm done mopping the hall. That's it."

With that, he heavily slumps down on the wheelchair – so heavily in fact, that one of the wheels gives way and breaks off. Of course, as a logical and direct consequence, J.F. instantly topples to one side, eyes widening while he's still in midair, mouth opened on a silent scream: nosediving on a vertical, he falls smack onto the concrete floor. Inexplicably but fortunately unhurt, he bounces right back up again, embarrassed to have fallen in front of me.  He picks up the wheelchair and screams:

"You FUCKING piece of SHIT!!!"

As I watch him, astounded, he lifts the chair completely over his head.  Now displaying superhuman strength, J.F. walks over to the end of the hall, still pallbearing the chair as he resolutely heads for the doors leading out to the service yard.  I get up and follow him, arriving just in time to see him kicking the doors wide open with a maniacal flick of the boot.  Then, mustering all his might, he swings against aim and catapults the chair straight into the Community Center's big industrial trash container.  We both watch as the item falls backwards in a spectacularly loud and dislocated finale, its wheels flying every which way, its stuffing knocked out and falling again in a gentle flurry of white foam bits.  While I stay there, petrified, J.F. looks on, emptied, his halting breath spurting out of his dilated nostrils.

One moment later, I lose it and burst out laughing.  As J.F. looks at me, startled, I just laugh and laugh.  I can't help it.  J.F. takes another look at the demolished chair, still pitifully jutting out from the container.  He starts to chuckle too and soon we're having one of those protracted, contagious, gushing laughing fits.  With the back of his hand, J.F. wipes the tears from his eyes as we go back inside.

"Oh shit, Laurie.  What's Giles gonna say?  I totally destroyed the wheelchair…"

"Just leave it there."

J.F. looks at me, grateful but still hesitant.  I try to reassure him completely:

"I'll tell Giles we came into the office and it was gone, that's all."

"What if he checks the bin?"

"I'll tell him I don't know how it got there."

"Really? You'd actually lie for me?"

"Yes, my good man."

"I wonder if he'll believe you…"

"Sadly, I'm one of his best, most trusted employees. And so are you. So that's that."

Back in the tank, J.F. sits on the floor, where the wheelchair used to be. I take up Kafka where I left him, between two scribbled margins.

"What's that book about?"

"It's the story of a guy who turns into a cockroach."

"No kidding?"

"None. I have to write a paper on it and I don't know how to start."

"I already handed in all my essays."

"Lucky you…"

"Oh, I forgot to rinse out the mop. If Giles finds it like that, I'm dead."

Even though he's our boss, and technically a white-collar, Giles never shrinks from taking up blue-collar duties whenever they're called for. The Community Center is his territory; he inspects it assiduously every day, even if he's the last one out at night and the first one in in the morning.

J.F. leaves, picking up his mop and bucket along the way. He walks towards the back of the building with a new spring in his step. It did him a lot of good, pulverizing that wheelchair. It's almost like he was an invalid, miraculously cured, going through a "get up and walk" kind of resurrection, a man taking his chair, his crutch or his handicap and throwing it away, far away, off in the distance, far from himself, over and beyond his illness.  A real live "metamorphosis", for sure.

Which gives me an idea...

## 30

I've finally managed to concoct a pretty good essay on Kafka, which was directly inspired by J.F.'s brief but brutal existential crisis. Feeling magnanimous, I've even decided to attend my last Poetry class all the way through, even staying on after the break.

The last class. Not the last class of the day, not the last class of the week or the last class before midterm. No. The very last class, the last last class of all classes. That class happens sooner than you think. You're stuck somewhere in the dead of school, you're fed up, you can't take it anymore, each week's like a month, each day's like a week, slow, interminable, never-ending, incessant, and then, all of a sudden, ping!, there you are: the last class. When I got up this morning, it felt like every minuscule, minute, microscopic part of my being was exploding from pure and utter joy. I think I've said "Yes sir!" about fifty times before leaving the house. In the train, I'm so excited, I can barely sit still. When Ticket-Ticket comes along, I talk to him for ten minutes straight, with no gaps. In school, in the corridors, I literally walk on air, gliding, floating so far above myself that people are actually staring. I even hum a little. Doing that, especially here, takes some nerve.

In class however, things, somehow, change. Every time the teacher finishes a sentence, I grumble to myself, lamenting wearily between clenched teeth. Three hours like that is a long time. I don't know what's going on; it's like the teacher thinks she can ramble on and on, on any stupid subject, just because it's the last class for her too and she doesn't have anything left to prove either; her course has been given, followed, endured and completed. She strolls in front of her desk, babbling away, looking happy and giddy, decked out in a loose bright-red shawl that falls floppily over flower-patterned pants: she looks like she's wearing gift-wrapping paper. I glance at my essay on Kafka. It's just sitting there, top of the pile, on her desk.

While I'm still mentally adrift, the teacher ventures out, moving among us through the aisles:

"In the last few weeks, some of you came to my office to tell me how much you were enjoying this class, how much it meant to you and how important it was in your academic progress."

Really? Who's the brownnoser? Who would be dumb enough to actually think that and then tell the teacher about it too? On my right, Trifocals is smiling radiantly. My God! Trifocals! He's the culprit! That's why she's been gratefully monologuing at us for the past ten minutes! He's the one who's been trying to score some extra points!

"I'm so happy you all participated in this class, and with such devotion…"

Good God.

"…so happy, in fact, that I thought I would end this class with a flourish."

Uh-oh.

"I thought it would be fun to review each student's contribution, one by one."

Oh no! I thought the whole thing was over, I thought I didn't have to worry anymore! I came here just to be polite! I thought I was out of range, safe!

Trifocals fidgets expectantly on his chair, like a puppy watering at the mouth. I, on the other hand, have been taken over by rigor mortis. "Review each student's contribution"? What does that mean, exactly?

"I've looked again at all your poems, I've read them all over again, and prepared for each of you a little summary of your journey here."

The teacher takes out her notes, about thirty pages. With a little hop, she sits on her desk, cross-legged, surprising all of us with her spontaneous breach of decorum. Sitting like that, relaxed, luminous with happiness, she actually looks pretty.

"I'll start with Andrew."

She glances over at Trifocals, whose body language now translates into joyful tail-wagging.

"Andrew, you displayed a tremendous amount of generosity throughout your creative process. Your poems were always original, with imaginative puns and a vocabulary that reveals a great, consistent love of exactitude. Your future is, I'm sure, extremely promising. Thank you for your wonderfully meticulous input. I read your work with great pleasure."

Trifocals, or rather Andrew, is beaming wide; his glasses almost fog up. I myself have to admit: the teacher's initiative is surprising. What with all the trouble she went through to prepare this, you'd think she was actually sincere.

"All right. Moving on to Fadia now."

On my left, Fadia is still doodling horribly. When the teacher calls out her name, she looks up, her eyes like saucers.

"Fadia, your poems really moved me. You are so sensitive, so vulnerable, your words always revealed something extremely personal. I was very touched to see how you were able to communicate your deepest, most intimate feelings with but a few delicate words. Thank you for your tenderness, your emotions, and the trust you placed in me."

Fadia, who like all of us listened intently to the teacher's assessment of her work, starts weeping gently, almost calmly. She wipes her cheeks with her sleeves and smiles thankfully at the teacher, who gives her an enveloping look. The moment is actually really moving; my chest is all constricted, but it's mostly from shame. I'm beginning to hate myself for being so prejudiced, for judging without knowing, for being so generally stupid. I'd like to take Fadia and Andrew in my arms, embrace them and tell them I'm sorry, but the teacher clears her throat before speaking again:

"Laurie."

Under the desk, my legs go limp. Over the desk, my heart pumps so hard I can hear it in my ears. I should've stayed home, dear God.

"Laurie, in all your poems, there is this loud, rebellious voice. There is anger, seething within… but there is also a true, deep sadness. What you wrote made me think about many things, it made me reflect on my own life. Sometimes, your words made me laugh, but they also exasperated me, surprised and upset me. I found in them the pleasure of letting myself be destabilized, challenged. Thank you for your forthrightness, for your blunt outlook on life and your absolute frankness."

I smile, a little perplexed by what I'm hearing; I don't even know if my work was good or not. The teacher lets out a chuckle, then shakes her head:

"Not easy…"

The other students laugh along with her, like a chorus, while she moves on to someone else.

What just happened here? I'm not sure. Was my work any good? "Not easy"? What does that mean? I don't even know how to process that comment! While the teacher goes on reviewing the rest of the class, I look at my essay on Kafka again, topping the pile on her desk. It's true. I wrote my poems on the fly, on high alert, prematurely angry, mostly because I've been rebelling against school essays in general. Writing for school is just so partial. Essays, by definition, are airtight and therefore airless; there's no room for choice of theme, for structure, sequence, unfolding or even word juxtaposition. Essays are always written slantwise, at an angle, with the teacher's expectations in sight. An essay can't help being obvious, with its exposed subject and vacillating level of interest, its sentences always mindful of being corrected, rectified, graded. Even before the first spelling mistake hatches, an essay knows it's being judged, it's already competing against what could be said, what should be said, and how.

So I guess it's hard to tell whether what I wrote was good or not. And I guess it's not really important to find out what the teacher thinks, or what all my other professors think, for that matter. What matters is contribution. And effort. That's about it. In the grand scheme of things, I at least made the effort to speak my mind, to bring ideas to the table, to contribute a thought in the endless flux of other thoughts. That's got to be important.

I look at the teacher again. She's talking to another student, draped in her colorful shawl and pants. I watch her as she speaks with generosity, with love for her profession, with patience for her students, and I smile at her when her eyes glide over me, mentally sending her loads and masses of thank-yous. I'm glad, really. I think it all ends well, all things considered. And even if I get a weak grade for that Kafka paper, and even though I've hated my time at school, and even if Larry and Cyn are eternally happy, or my father remains distant and negligent, or I'm still single and often sigh long into the night, I'd say overall the scales tip out of the red. Not bad. I'm happy. I'm okay. Because even though school is not quite over yet, I'm already out of it, outside, free, done with my degree and all things obligatory. What's more, I don't even harbor one ounce of resentment against anybody or anything, no hatred or vindictiveness of any kind. I didn't like going to university. That's true. But there will always be other students that love it and make it worthwhile, and give universities their God-given right to exist.

Thirty minutes later, it happens. The teacher looks at her watch, sighs, and starts saying "Well, I guess that's it. I wish you…" My brain's so busy smiling, laughing, exulting, being swept away by full ecstasy, that I never hear the end of that sentence. All I know is class is over. Gently now, surrounded by the other students as they leave, I get up, take my school bag, pick up my coat, put on my scarf, ease my chair back under the desk, say "Goodbye" to Andrew and Fadia, and step out! WOO-

HOO!  I'M DONE!  IT'S OVER!!  SCHOOL'S OUT FOREVER!!!  Yes!

After those first few minutes where I thought I was going to have a fit from extreme exaltation, skipping everywhere in the subway, telling strangers left and right "I'm graduating!", a weird feeling comes over me. Something like a vague and vaporous question rears up, something that sounds like a sly little "What now?" that almost passively snips my happiness in half, in the background, on the quiet.  No, no, Laurie, please, two more minutes, give yourself at least two lousy minutes before asking yourself "What now?"  Two minutes of unsurpassable joy, two minutes of pristine plenitude, devoid of doubts and questions.  Please, just two minutes…

Of course, one cannot change one's nature.

When the subway gets underway, I ask myself where I should send my résumé.  And what should I write in it?  I mean, I never did anything in life, really.  What if instead of starting, life ended right here, right now?  What if that was it: no more experiences, no more partying, no desire left to live life to the fullest, no dreams of changing someone else's existence through mine, no need to tell myself bad moments are just moments that pass.  Yes, this is it.  It's the end.  The end of an era, the end of days, of dreams and hopes mixed together, the end of the idea that it only takes one more day to begin all over again…

All of a sudden, I start to smile.  Yes, I smile right there, smack dab in the middle of the subway.  Picking up my school bag, holding it tight, pressed up against my chest, I speak in a soft voice, like a wishful whisper:

"So what?"